I0761826

The Women With Blue Eyes

Rise Of The Fallen

An Urban Fantasy Novel

YECHEILYAH YSRAYL

For information contact:

www.yecheilyahysrayl.com

yecheilyah@yecheilyahysrayl.com

First Edition: 2021

Contents

CHAPTER ONE

Friday, December 31, 2004, 11:58a

632 N. Dearborn St., Excalibur Castle

Chicago Dance Club

Bodies filled all five levels of the massive venue, and the music growled from the belly of the loudspeakers. Excalibur once again managed to stuff every available body into the three-level club. Blue, green, red, and yellow lights beamed from above the DJ table and hung from the second and third floors, illuminating the pack of intoxicated bodies on the ground floor.

"Erica girl, where you been? It's about to start."

Tina turned away from the bar to face her friend. Her body filled out the black dress as the woman waved her hot face.

“What?”

Tina laughed; the women couldn’t hear themselves over the music.

“It’s about to start. The countdown!” yelled Tina in Erica’s ear.

“Wait, lemme get my drink.”

“Girl, please. Time don’t wait for nobody. You better c’mon.”

Tina jumped down from the barstool.

“Grey Goose martini and plain cranberry juice,” shouted Erica to the bartender who smiled and winked.

A crowd of people began to surround the main stage as it prepared to lower the huge crystal ball to the middle of the floor.

“I need ya’ll to make some noise,” the emcee’s voice boomed from the microphone, sending the crowd into hysteria.

“C’mon E,” said Tina, watching as Erica wobbled her five-foot frame through the crowd. The women stumbled toward the stage, laughing.

“Here we go!” yelled the DJ.

“Woo-hoo” yelled Tina, laughing. It had been a long time since she had this much fun.

“I love you, Chicago!” screamed Erica.

Tina laughed. She was tripping on that drink.

"We love you!"

"I love you, too baby," said the DJ.

"Woo-hoo," laughed Erica and Tina.

"Ten…nine…" began the DJ.

"Eight…" said Erica.

"Seven…" said Tina.

"Six…" said the crowd.

As the crowd sang along, something caught Tina's eye. A man, wearing a black suit and tie, reserved more for the courtroom than the club, stood in the distance. The sound around her went mute and her mind raced to determine the strange man's identity.

Tina spent the last year in therapy, trying to forget about her traumatic past. She had not expected to walk into Erica's office to receive such a down to Earth reality check from a doctor who was now dancing out her dress in a club with her. As such, Tina took this as a sign that things were finally back to normal, taking hallucinogenic suppressants as prescribed, and even cutting off any ties to the former life. But now, as the club lights bounced off the hint of blue that glowed even in the darkness, she knew it was him again. She could never understand why he always seemed to be hiding. It's not like anyone else could see him.

"HAPPY NEW YEAR!"

The crowd's shout forced Tina to take a step back. Erica hugged her and spilled some of her drink.

"Damn, messing with you."

Tina smiled to conceal her changed demeanor, but it was too late.

"Hey girl, you alright?"

Tina's eyes darted frantically around the club for the man, but he was gone.

"Yeah, girl. I'm good," she said waving her hand.

"You sure? You been taking the pills, right? Don't let me have to write yo butt up."

Tina stole one more glance in the direction where the man once stood, but there was no one there.

"Yeah, girl. I'm alright," Tina waved. "Where's the bathroom, though?" she said with laughter to fake the fear that already started to grow the tiny hairs on her skin, the sweat already creeping its way down her back. Tina gripped her purse as Erica pointed in the direction of the ladies' room. She was definitely in need of a double dose tonight.

CHAPTER TWO

Byron brushed the lint from his uniform as he approached the home of his last client of the day. Walking up the steps, he noticed the beautiful brick home in the well-groomed neighborhood. *Must be HOA*, he thought. Homeowners associations had these affluent white neighborhoods looking like no one lived in the houses, and whoever lived in them certainly had no children. The grass is always a vibrant green and cut in perfect lines. There is no trash on the sidewalks, and although he saw dogs and cats, even their poop wasn't visible. *Damn.* Byron knocked on the door and looked down at his paperwork.

"Yes?"

The door swung open, and a woman smiled back at him.

"Good afternoon ma'am my name…"

Byron paused, mesmerized. The woman's skin was dark chocolate, her hair so silky black it looked fake, her lips thick and plush with a coat of the reddest lipstick he'd ever seen, and she wore those childbearing hips well. But none of that had anything on her eyes. The woman had the most beautiful blue eyes he'd ever seen. Strange against such cocoa butter skin. He could look right through them. Byron cleared his throat. A woman had never had him so caught off guard.

"My name is Byron Fisher with Guaranteed Insurance Company. We have you listed as requesting a return visit." Byron held up a hand. "I know. I'm not the guy from last time, but you were on my route, so I thought I'd stop by and see which plan might interest you," he smiled.

"Oh, yes," said the woman, her voice soft and delicate.

Damn, thought Byron, his manhood growing. He'd better get it together quick. The khaki pants he wore today wouldn't do much to hide the excitement. He cursed himself for not deciding on jeans.

She could hear his thoughts, and she smiled despite herself. She could see in more than one direction as she read Byron's energy. Her eyes were cameras quickly processing the environment. They zoomed in on the car coming up the street, the lady walking her dog on the corner, and the mailman who was late again. Even the candy wrapper in the cracks of the concrete, if she concentrated harder, she could make out the image of the child who dropped it there while waiting for the school bus to arrive.

Byron's biography flashed against the screens that were her eyes. It told her he was single with no children and plenty of money to spend. He was also an orphan as a child and moved around a lot before enlisting in the military. After the army, Byron got into the insurance business. Life never looked better. Well, almost never. The woman smiled. She saw his weakness, too, his hurt.

He was in love once. Some detective woman he couldn't have because she dated his friend. The woman's eyes flashed. She was digging. The chief warned of *digging*. It required the use of too much energy, but she had to know. So, she searched. Her eyes clawed his eyes for secrets. It was safe. At least now. He couldn't feel anything…not yet.

Byron wiped at his brow, frowning at the sudden wave of heat on his face.

The woman smiled, the flashing red dots on the screen of her eyes, signaling the passion emanating from the man in front of her. He wanted her. This would be easy. She stopped *digging* before he fainted in broad daylight. The chief wouldn't have that again.

"Very nice to meet you," said the woman. "I am sure we can find *something* that I like. Please, come in."

Byron smiled as he walked into the home of the beautiful blue-eyed woman. He couldn't believe his luck. Some women were easy. Maybe he'll get her to sign off on more than just papers. He smiled, and her blue eyes flashed, a smirk on her face as she closed the door behind him.

CHAPTER THREE

"Ronnie, no!"

Tina snatched her robe from the hook on the door and pulled it tight around her body. She was in Janiyah's room. There was no explanation needed, and no sound escaped either of their mouths except the whispering words of comfort coming from Tina.

"Shh. It's alright now. It's alright. It's over."

She rocked and rubbed the young woman's head with her eyes closed. This was her routine, running into Janiyah's room in the early mornings, though she didn't think it would have lasted this long. She also worried she could not sympathize with her best friend's daughter, now her own. To lose your baby brother in such a violent way was one thing; to witness his murder was another thing. And then, there was the *other* thing.

Tina's cell was singing in the room downstairs. Peering down at her exhausted teenager, she quickly untangled her body and let the girl fall back into the sheets, covering her before running downstairs, into her bedroom, and silencing the phone before it woke up the other kids.

Hmm. Tina looked down at the tiny screen. That was odd. What was the office doing calling her so early?

She looked toward the window. She still couldn't believe the city had settled. The money helped her buy a bigger house to raise his brother and sisters, but it was still too big. No amount of money could bring her nephew back. The money was good. She couldn't lie. It felt good not to worry about bills or pray she didn't have to investigate some asshole to make ends meet.

Tina loved this time of day. Early, when the sky was still dark. She threw herself back into the bed and called the office.

"You better have a damn good reason for calling me so early in the morning."

"What?"

Tina's smile faded, and she sat up in the bed. "When did this happen?" She got out of bed and balanced the cordless phone between her ear and shoulder as she slipped on a pair of pants. Trying to do the same with a blouse was not going to work.

"Hold on a minute..."

Placing the phone on the bed, she slipped on her shirt and put the phone on speaker.

"The phones are blowing up over here. Officer Parks said she started getting them as early as last night," said the caller.

"Calls? What calls? I thought I told you to hold. Fred had a bad habit of checking out, staring off in space. Tina was sure he was staring off when she told him to hold on. She picked up a sock and put it on. Now if she could just find the other one.

Tina wasn't the organized type at home. What she could do at the office did not manifest in her private life. It was one of the worries she had about being a mom. Detectives didn't exactly have a lot of time on their hands. She found herself hiring a nanny against her better judgment to help maintain that balance. She had little time for laundry and housework, and now that Janiyah had her license, she could pick up her brother and sister from school. She did make it a point to be back in time to make dinner and spend time with the kids. It made her feel motherly, like she was upholding her end of the bargain. Miss Bernice was not allowed to cook for her family except on occasion and during emergencies. This sounded like one of them.

"All I know is you better get your butt down here asap."

"I'm on my way," said Tina looking under the bed. *Where in the world is that other sock?*

"Yeah, I know what that means. I'll give you an hour."

"Freddy, chill. I said I'm on my way."

"Your *on-the-way* has a different meaning from everyone else's," Fred chuckled.

Tina rolled her eyes and hung up on her partner.

"Kayla…Michael…Niyah," she called, climbing the stairs and walking the length of the hall. She peered into the room she was just in before the call.

"Janiyah, ya'll come on. I need ya'll to get up."

The young woman stirred and sat up, a black night scarf covering her head. Her elegantly arched eyebrows shot up.

"What time is it?"

Tina smirked. She didn't know how she did it, but Janiyah managed to be cute at every occasion, even after waking up. The nose ring she begged Tina for didn't look bad against her golden-brown skin.

"I need you to call Miss Bernice. Tell her I need her to come in early. Like, right now."

"Okay." Janiyah patted her head. "Where's your other sock at?" she laughed.

Tina cut her eyes as she turned away from the room and ran back downstairs, calling names as she descended.

"Mike, KK. Up. Now!"

As she hurried, her mind flooded with Fred's urgent message.

Another man was found dead yesterday in the Cicero neighborhood of 145th Avenue, now the fifth black man to die in the past seven days. It happened the same as the others, in broad daylight. All the men were found dead in hotel rooms or their own homes, suffocated. The latest death is the oddest of them all. Some insurance company worker found dead on the floor in the bedroom of an empty house. He was still wearing his blue-collar insurance shirt and khaki pants. Tina thought about this as she grabbed her purse, walked down to the house's main level, and grabbed her keys off the kitchen counter. She hated cases like this. They made her think of *them*. Tina froze on her way to the door. How could she have forgotten the most crucial piece of the puzzle? Ronnie.

Ronnie lost his life in a drug deal gone wrong last year. There was a shootout at an empty warehouse where his sisters and brother were kidnapped and held hostage. Ronnie's loyalty to Big Sam, the dealer who hired him, ultimately cost him his life. But Tina knew the truth. It was the year everything began, the increase in deaths, and the UFO sightings all over the world. Tina knew better. *They* had killed him. *Is that why the city had awarded the settlement money? Who would want to admit the impossible was possible? That they did come but were not the friendly miracle workers we thought they would be? Was her team trying to sweep the truth under the rug?*

Tina walked out of the door as her body trembled. She knew Big Sam had blue eyes, and Ronnie's death was no accident. They had murdered her nephew, were back, and killing again.

CHAPTER FOUR

"Aliens?"

"Look, laugh all you want. I am *not* crazy."

Erica composed herself.

"I'm sorry, girl. You sound like you believe it, and if you believe, I do too, but…"

"Then you don't believe me."

Tina got up from the sofa and walked over to Erica's downtown office window, where she could see the Sears Tower, the third-tallest building in the United States and the Western hemisphere—and the twenty-third-tallest in the world. Downtown Chicago was one of the most beautiful places in the country, known for its beautiful skylines and iconic skyscrapers.

Erica put her notepad to the side.

"Okay. Let's entertain this for a moment. You gotta think about how this is going to sound. Your nephew died in a drug deal…"

"…it wasn't a drug deal," interrupted Tina turning around. It pissed her off people were still saying that.

"Hold on. Let me finish. Far as *they* know it, your nephew dies in a drug deal, and everyone else flees the scene. You take leave from work to raise Keisha's kids, your remaining nieces, and nephew who, by the way, aren't really your nieces and nephew…"

"Erica…"

"You take them in after winning a custody battle with their dad after he couldn't prove stable residency and their drug addict mom permitted you to have them. And now, everyone involved in the case is tied to you in some way. Top this all off with the death of another black man by God knows who and your claim that aliens killed Ronnie and abducted everyone at the Warehouse."

Tina nodded. It did sound crazy when you said it out loud. She sat on the sofa, resting her head on the pillow behind her.

"I'm not saying I don't believe you, but you a detective girl. You should know this ain't gonna stick."

"So, what am I to do then? I can't keep taking these pills. It's driving me crazy."

"Listen, you need these pills so you can do your job without seeing little blue men walking around."

"That's not funny E."

"Seriously, here's what I think. Here's my professional opinion…"

Tina smirked. "Now you wanna be professional?"

"Don't be in my office judging me," laughed Erica, "I'm the one with the pen. In my *professional* opinion, I think you should see if you can find a connection between those who were abducted and people who may be working with these aliens or whatever around here killing folk. They gotta be working with somebody, or they wouldn't be able to do anything without being seen."

Tina sat up.

"They look like men, though, like humans. That's how they can move about without notice. It's not like in the movies."

"Still, they gotta be working with everyday people. Find those people."

Tina looked at Erica and bit her lip. It was a start.

"Meanwhile," Erica stood and walked over to her desk and tore off a piece of paper. She walked back to the sofa and handed it to Tina.

"Get it together."

Tina rolled her eyes and took the prescription.

"I don't need it."

"Yes, you do. Even if it's just in case."

***

Tina thought deeply about Erica's words on the drive home. She did have her wheels turning. *Who could be involved in something like this?* Tina laughed. *This some conspiracy theory shit*. Reaching for the folders, she scanned the names again. Chareese, Antonio, Brandon, Sidney, Emmanuel. They were all her friends and all reported missing at precisely the same time as Ronnie's death. Someone was missing, though. Tina tapped her fingers against the steering wheel. Her close ties to everyone abducted at the warehouse did make her look suspicious, so she had to be careful.

Tina went to high school with Ja'mella back in the day, who had started talking to some cat from the hood named Antonio, who everyone called Tony. Ja'mella came back into Tina's life when she filed a rape charge against Tony and his best friend Brandon, who was in a committed relationship with Tina's friend Chareese at the time. Chareese was also pregnant with Brandon's baby. The case centered around ties to Big Sam, the largest drug queenpin in Chicago. Big Sam sparked something with Tina's sister-friend Keisha and got her strung out. Keisha couldn't pay her debt to Sam, and that's how her son Ronnie got involved. Sam recruited him to work off his mama's debt. They were all connected in a "six degrees of separation" kind of way.

Tina searched her thoughts, remembering their card games and get-togethers. They had all been tight at some point or another. Though she knew them all personally, she wasn't really tight with the men, and the women had gone their separate ways until the case united them.

Tina pressed the button on her dashboard to connect her bluetooth to the speaker and waited as it rang. Only one person was missing from the crew. A click sounded, and Fred answered the phone.

"Yeap."

"Hey, Fred? What did you say the name of that insurance guy was?"

Tina's face froze as Fred gave her the name.

"Tina? T, you there?"

"Yeah, yeah. I'm here. Thanks."

Tina pressed the button to hang up, still in shock. She had forgotten all about King.

King was another one of Antonio's friends from college. He had a big crush on her back in the day, but she went to a different school, and he joined the military. She hadn't seen him since then. His real name was Byron, and now he was dead.

CHAPTER FIVE

The woman moved her hips from side to side on her way to the kitchen, and the man cleared his throat, watching as her booty swayed underneath the red silk skirt. There was something about dark skin against red. Baby girl was all body. He shook his head, trying to focus as the sweat began to trickle down the side of his face. He loosened the collar on his shirt. *Damn, it's hot in here.*

"Aye Mama, you got something cold to drink in here?"

He wiped his brow and dried his sweaty hands off on his post office jeans. Something told him not to be greedy and try to do one more block, but when he saw those beautiful blue eyes, he couldn't resist. They were light blue and a tad bit creepy but also a tad bit sexy. The woman returned with a large pitcher of tea and a glass. The guy wondered how she could hold both without dropping them.

Damn she strong.

The woman smiled, handing him the glass and holding the pitcher with both hands as she poured the sweet liquid. Her breasts dangled in front of her guest.

"It's been quite warm lately," she said licking her lips and smiling.

Jason watched the show. He wasn't much of a breast man. They weren't as much fun as booty and thighs. "Titties are for babies," he told his friends. But he damn sure wasn't complaining. He watched them jiggle when she sat down.

"How long have you been in this house? I don't remember seeing you around here, and I been working this route for a minute," he emptied his glass. It really must have been hot because he only drank like that when he was super thirsty.

"Oh, I'm new here."

The blue-eyed woman moved closer, staring into his eyes. Her skin didn't have a wrinkle, spot, or blemish. It was like someone had painted her skin brown. The man thought that was kind of weird, but his hormones told him to ignore it as the woman's hips touched his.

She watched the red spots on the internal screen of her eyes as Jason's temperature rose. He loosened his collar and cleared his throat, then leaned in closer to the woman, his lips so close to hers she could feel his cool breath on her face. The woman smiled and continued to stare into his eyes.

"Digging for souls again?"

Startled, the woman turned in the voice's direction and back to the man, whose mouth hung open, his body stiff. She turned around to the being who spoke, her eyes rigid and cold, her jaw clenched.

"You froze him?"

"He'll snap out of it in a second. Won't remember a thing," said the being.

The woman sighed. She hated when they froze time. She folded her arms.

"What are you doing here? This isn't exactly your jurisdiction."

"Pas, you don't need to do this. Haven't you had enough already?"

Paschar stood and walked toward the being. The archangel stood eight feet and wore Hispanic skin. Paschar shook her head at the suit and tie he wore. He looked like one of *them*.

"Good and man is an oxymoron. I know how badly you want to be one of them. Are you a good *man* Az?"

"Stop playing games. I have orders from the Almighty. You can't touch him."

"See, Az, that's the difference between you and me. You are a sheep, blindly following your master." She laughed, walking back to the sofa, and waved her hand in the face of the stiff man before her.

"They are *so* weak, it's pathetic. I tell you what. You can have him if I can have *her*."

Az thought about seeing her at the club the other night. They hadn't spoken since last year when he first showed himself. She seemed frightened of him, and he didn't want her to be afraid. Fear would stop her from completing the mission he had arrived to give her. Fear would dim the light that would save Jason's life.

"That's not how this works. You know that."

"Oh," Paschar bit her lip in a fake pout. "That sucks."

"I'm not playing games with you Paschar. Stop digging or I disintegrate you."

"Ouch. Pulling out the big guns, huh? I can do stuff too, you know?"

"This isn't a competition. There are people's lives at stake here."

Paschar spun around in a fury, appearing behind Az in seconds. He was used to this and didn't budge.

"Exactly. People. Ungrateful, weak-minded human beings care about nothing but themselves, their fancy cars, and worthless money. They can't even breathe on their own, let alone 'control their own destiny.' Bunch of weak-minded fools is what they are." She folded her arms across her chest. It pissed her off that despite being more powerful than humans, her legion still didn't have a chance at redemption.

"You stop digging or I turn you in, and you *know* what that means."

"I don't have to listen to you."

"There's a bottomless pit with your name on it. Try me."

The archangel vanished and the man snapped out of his trance and shook his head. The woman was standing.

Was it over already? I know I ain't that desperate I can't remember hitting it.

Paschar walked over to the door and opened it.

"You can leave now."

***

Tina tightened the nightcap on her head and sighed. It had been a long day at the office trying to solve the Byron case. The children were with her mother for the weekend, and Janiyah was at a friend's house, albeit she was on curfew and due back soon. In any event, the house was empty. Tina was thankful for that, at least. She needed the break.

Tina turned over on her side and pulled the tiny chain on the lamp, but it wouldn't turn off. She pulled again—still, nothing.

"Come on now." Tina removed the covers and stood over the lamp. She pulled the chain again, but the light wouldn't turn off.

"Gotta be these cheap ass bulbs. Told Mama not to get this brand."

"Don't be afraid."

"Ahh!"

Tina picked up the lamp and threw it at the tall odd-looking man standing in her bedroom. She jumped on the bed and backed into the corner, holding her chest, her breathing heavy.

"I am sorry to approach you this way, but I need to talk to you."

"Ahh!"

"Please, stop screaming."

"Janiyah!"

"No one's here."

Tina's heart raced as she remembered she did have the house to herself.

"I am sorry, but I knew no other way to visit you."

Tina first started seeing Az when Ronnie died, before her boss recommended she see Erica. It had happened right there at the office. She was snitched on by Amy, her rival, who caught her *talking to herself.* She knew it was him that night at the club but did not want to admit it to herself.

"So, you *are* following me."

"It's kind of important."

Tina looked him up and down.

"Are you all blue?"

His full name was Azbuga meaning 'Strength.'

The angel frowned, "What?"

"Is your whole body blue or is it just your eyes?"

"I don't really look like a human. This is the image I show you, so you're not afraid."

Tina crawled across the bed and inched closer, settled in the middle of the bed, and folded her arms.

"Well, it didn't work."

"Listen, it's gonna happen again," he said giving Tina a folder. She took it and opened it.

"Her name's Paschar, the angel of vision, but we call her Pas for short. She's a sinister entity who sucks the souls of black men right out of them using her eyes."

Tina dropped the folder like it had burned her hand, "Nope."

"I have not even explained it to you."

"I've heard enough. The whole entities and sucking souls from black men shit. Nope."

"There is no one else. This is your time."

Tina rolled her eyes, "My time for what?"

"To develop your light."

Tina sighed and reached again for the folder. Maybe if she entertained his shenanigans, he would leave her alone. Of all the angels she imagined as a kid, irritating was not part of that description. Nigga didn't even have wings.

Not all angels have wings.

Tina looked up from the folder, "You reading my thoughts now?"

"Please, just look at the file."

Tina stared at a woman's photo.

"She's beautiful."

"Exactly the problem. Pas kills more men than anyone of her kind. There are many of them. She's high up there."

Tina flipped another page and looked over the paperwork, stopping at a black man's photo. He smiled wide, showing a row of beautiful white teeth. Not many men smile like this for pictures. They all do the mean mug as if there was something wrong with a black man smiling. Tina laughed at the audacity of the man's set-apartness. He wore an Afro and a blue Chicago Bears t-shirt. He was handsome, and she caught herself staring.

"His name is Jason. I stopped her before she did anything, but Paschar can't be trusted. She's going to cross me and..."

He nodded toward the photo in Tina's hands.

"…and kill him."

"Why?"

Tina stared at Az, no longer frightened by his appearance. He was taller than a normal man but could shorten his height around people like he did that night at the club. He was at least eight feet in this form, and Tina found herself looking up to talk to him.

"Why me? Why black men? Why now?"

"Energy."

Tina rolled her eyes, "Okay, now tell me the real reason."

"Energy. Paschar and her crew are fallen angels, no longer connected with the Master…"

"God? When you say Master, you mean God?"

"Listen, they need the energy and worship from humans to live. There's a connection to you because Ronnie's involvement with one of their kind opened a door. The more men Paschar and her girls take out, the longer they live. Sexual energy is one of the most powerful forms of energy there is. Your sexual energy is a creative, lifeforce energy. Through it, you give birth to a new life, and the fallen watcher angels have always been jealous of that."

"Angels jealous of humans having babies? Get outta here," laughed Tina.

"Not all angels, but the fallen watchers for sure. Ever since Mount Herman." Az paused reflectively.

"Okay, but why *black* men? Every victim has so far been black, considering this has to do with the deaths we are finding all over the city. Is it because she's black?"

"Paschar is not African American. She appears that way, same as I appear to you as an Hispanic man. I know your father was Hispanic, so you wouldn't fear me in this form. We angels do not have a race, color, or human form. We are energy."

"Why *black* men though?" Tina asked again, annoyed he had not answered her question.

"Paschar and her crew crave the sexual energy of black men because their power is the strongest of all races of men. It is a strong force that gives her legion longevity. Men are weakened by the sight of their physical beauty and sex appeal, and their weakness is a doorway they use to suck the energy from their eyes. Black men have one of the most potent energy forces there is. Black women follow them, and Black children follow you. It is the order of the universe. Listen, if Pas visits a man herself, he must be extraordinary. She saves the best for her. Jason is visiting his daughter at precisely two o'clock tomorrow. Afterward, he will stop at a friend's house for a short while before heading home. At this friend's house, they will meet a group of women. Beautiful women. Jason cannot be there. If he meets up with his friends at *any* time and for *any* reason, he is dead. Get to him before she does."

Az vanished.

"Wait!"

Tina punched the bed, then buried her face in the pillow and screamed. Her head was pounding like crazy. Why was this happening to her? Why had Ronnie's death invited angels and demons into her life? Her eyes looked ahead to the bathroom. Only now did she realized Az's large figure had blocked it entirely from view. Erica's pills were calling out to her, and so was the aspirin. She wouldn't see Az if she took the pills and wouldn't know what to do next. She did need those aspirin, though.

"Choices, choices."

She looked down on the bed at the envelope Az gave her with Jason's information in it. He was so beautiful, but she couldn't involve herself in this. She decided to take Erica's prescription over the aspirin. This was all too much. She touched Jason's picture, caressed his face, and sighed.

"Sorry, baby. But I'm not your savior."

CHAPTER SIX

"Higher Daddy, higher! Push me higher!"

The four-year-old swung her legs back and forth, feeling the wind on her face. Jason smiled. Amarie was a fun junkie like her daddy.

"I don't think you ready for this, though, Marie Baby. You ready for this?"

"I'm ready, I'm ready. Higher Daddy!"

Jason stopped the swing and placed his hands on each side. He stepped back, pulling Amarie back, high into the air, his hands still holding on tightly to the swing. Amarie laughed and giggled. Jason let go, letting the swing fly through the air as Marie screamed. Jason laughed.

"Told you you weren't ready!"

As the swing came back to him, he stopped it, helping Amarie to climb down.

"Come on, Baby. Let's go feed Daddy."

"That was amazing!" shrieked Amarie, still feeling giddy.

Jason smiled. Kids were something else. One minute they were asking you a million questions, and the next minute they were little geniuses.

"Amazing, huh? Spell it for Daddy."

Amarie twisted her lip, and Jason couldn't get over the cuteness. She was his little chocolate drop, her skin taking on her mother's dark complexion instead of his lighter one. Her brown, coarse hair was in ponytails with yellow barrettes adorning the braided ends. Jason and his baby mama didn't always get along, but he admired how she always kept his daughter fresh and looking like a little lady. Not too many little girls still wore pigtails these days. While Moms kept her cute, Jason kept her smart. He taught her beauty on the outside meant nothing without beauty on the inside. "And beauty," he instructed her, "come with brains. Don't just be a cutie. Be smart, too." She would perk up at that. "A smart cutie!" Jason would laugh. "Yes, a smart cutie."

"A-M-A…" began Amarie.

Jason tried hard to listen, but his spirit was still disturbed by the events of the other day. He wouldn't teach his daughter the importance of thinking if he weren't a thinking man. *I know for a fact she was sitting right next to me. How the hell did she end up on the other side of the room, standing up?* He couldn't remember what happened when he was about to kiss the woman when she put him out. Wanting to kiss her was also weird. He wasn't that kind of man. He didn't kiss women he didn't know. It was strange and had him feeling uneasy. *It was hot as hell in there, too, though,* he reasoned. *Could that have been the reason? Did I blackout from the heat?*

"N-G," recited Amarie as they made it to the car. Jason helped her into the back seat and strapped her into her booster.

"Did I do it right, Daddy?"

"Yeah, Baby. Good job."

He closed her door and felt a wave of heat on his neck. Frowning, Jason turned around before opening his car door and saw no one.

"Jay man, you are tripping."

"Tripping. T-R-I…" began Amarie.

Jason laughed, taking out his flip phone and entering the vehicle.

"I'm not gonna make it out that way any time soon, bro," boomed Jason's deep, melodic voice. He laughed into the phone.

Big Steve was always saying something crazy.

"Nah, nothing like that. I got the little one with me. Yeah. Ya'll go ahead, though. Imma stop by Moms, and I can leave her there and catch ya'll later. The steakhouse? Bet. I ain't eating, though. Jason paused as his friend admonished him on the other end.

"Because bro, you know Moms ain't gonna let me stop by and *not* eat!"

He laughed, hung up, and dialed another number.

"'Sup, old man. You at the crib? Oh, yeah? What she cook? Bet. I'm on my way. I got Marie with me. Aiight. See you soon."

Jason hung up and then strapped on his seat belt. Whatever it was he was feeling, he didn't trust it. He always talked things over with his dad. He felt fortunate to have him in his life still. Not many black men he knew could say they grew up with both parents in the home. Jason's parents had been married for twenty-five years. That meant something to him. It also made him ashamed that he couldn't hold onto a relationship himself. As Jason pulled out of his parking space and began to drive down the street, he prayed his mother's cooking could help to shake the cold chill that trickled down his spine and the knot that lingered in the pit of his stomach.

***

"Internet stalking your boyfriend? Sweetie, if you think he's cheating, he's cheating."

Amy laughed as she walked past Tina's cubicle, where she had pulled up a photo of Jason on her computer screen. Quickly, Tina opened another tab.

"It's not like that."

She shook her head and crossed out the word MySpace on her notepad. The man was invisible online, no social media of any kind. She did discover he had been working for the U.S. Postal Service for three years. Before that, he attended a community college but then dropped out. Anything before that was still a mystery. Tina tapped her pencil on the desk, still unsure if she should intervene, and because she had taken her prescription, there was no sign of Az to help. If she was going to help, she only had a few hours to do it, and she had no idea where this Jason dude was.

"Hey, Fred?"

"Yep?"

"Look up this name for me."

Fred took the Post-it from Tina and frowned.

"Jason King?"

Amy laughed, shaking her head.

Fred pressed, "Who's he?"

"With a name like Jason King, shid," laughed Amy.

Fred laughed, too. Tina shook her head.

"Ya'll play too much. I don't even know the guy. I think he may be connected to the Byron case."

Fred frowned, "In what way?"

"I don't know, but I think he's involved."

In the new browser she typed in her company password and pulled up Byron's file. Amy cut her eyes.

CHAPTER SEVEN

Paschar licked her lips and smoothed out the wrinkles in her skirt as she stepped over the body, closing the door behind her. The electricity from his soul caused her entire body to pulsate and the blue in her eyes to shine bright. The fresh human essence had her whole body shaking, like one giant orgasm bursting from every crevice of her body. She wanted to run, jump, leap into the air. Travel the planets and back down again. Her prowess and senses were magnified after each hit. Paschar walked with confidence and held her head high as she moved her hips from side to side. Red was her most favorite color to wear with this skin. Something about the hue against this dark body is so different from her true form and more comfortable to navigate the Earth. Who wanted to be invisible to humans when it was easier to seduce them in the skin of a beautiful black woman? Passersby, men and women alike, looked, and Paschar smiled. They always stared. Humans were fascinated by blue, crystal pupils against such brown, creamy skin. In real life, Pas thought human bodies were disgusting. She hated the soft, gooeyness of the flesh, how it bruised and bled so quickly, how it fell apart and crumbled with each passing day. She hated the rotting meat on the bone, but she did come to love dark skin tones. Other pigments didn't make her heart beat like melanin. With it, she could extend life in this body and still feel like the angelic entity she was. Every soul she consumed slowed the aging of the body.

Paschar entered El Che Steakhouse and Bar restaurant and followed the blue-ray that led to the booth in the corner where five women with blue eyes sat. They smiled, their ethnicities ranging from Korean to European and from Hispanic to Japanese. None of them were black like her. Only she had the privilege of wearing African skin.

She snapped her fingers, causing the patrons to freeze in their places. Forks, spoons, and knives floated in the air; waitresses stopped in mid-step with full trays, people froze while chewing, and children's smiles were frozen on their faces.

"Hello, ladies. By the look in your eyes, I can tell you're feeling what I'm feeling," smiled Paschar, shimmying her hips. The women laughed.

"Indeed," said the Japanese woman. She was most happy with her body. It was fun to know what life was like taller than six inches. She slapped high-fives with the European woman next to her.

“Don’t get too excited. Az is on our trail.”

The Puerto Rican blew a breath, “Su problema.”

“Az is a pain in my ass,” complained the Japanese woman.

“You need to eat,” continued Pas. “More than usual. Keep your energy up. Men, women. I don’t care what you have to do. Eat and live. The stronger the worship, the stronger we are in battle.”

The woman in European skin with the Russian accent rolled her eyes, “Yeah, *stronger the worship*. Except they don’t pray to us anymore.”

“If you were out there eating and filling up on blood, that wouldn’t make a difference. The more you eat, the stronger you’ll be.”

The other women hid their laughter. Everyone knew Sasha had fewer victims than the rest of them. She was a beast as a gargoyle, but she couldn’t get many black men to look her way in this city as a white woman.

“Can’t we just go to Ohio or something?”

The Korean shook her head. “How many black people you know are in Ohio? Chicago, New York, Los Angeles, Detroit, Miami, Atlanta, these are the hotspots. How many times we have to say it?”

"She's right," said Paschar, "Don't waste time in cities that do not serve us. We need these people eating out of the palm of our hands."

"Or our ass," laughed the Japanese woman.

Within seconds Paschar's arm stretched across the room, and her hand was wrapped around the woman's throat and choking her up against the wall. She had just had a hit, and her energy was intense. The woman squirmed and squealed as her face contorted, revealing snippets of her true fairy image.

"You have forgotten what is at stake here," Paschar addressed the table. "There is no redemption for us. Semjaza is gone." Pas felt the anger rise in her throat at the mention of her leader.

"Arakiba," she continued, giving the names of their leaders. "Gone! Rameel, Kokabiel, Baraqijal, Armaros, gone. All of them!" Paschar slammed her fist against the table, and the women jumped. The Japanese woman continued to squirm as she suffocated against the wall.

"Two hundred of our fathers fell that day."

She let the Japanese woman go, her human body falling to the floor, coughing and choking.

Paschar walked the length of the restaurant, zooming in and out of focus, floating from one end of the room to the next, the anger in her veins amplified by the energy from her last victim.

"Their eternal souls locked away until their essence burns forever." Her voice grew more resonant, and black wings grew out of her shoulders. "They failed," she boomed, her voice like thunder.

"We will not fail. Rise sistars. Rise!"

The women stood, their body changing, disfiguring the human flesh, now like clay, and exposing their actual images. No longer were they five beautiful women, all ranging in skin tones and nationality. Now she looked into the face of a mermaid, a fairy, a white-winged horse, a gargoyle, and an imp.

Paschar had changed, too. Her real body was pale and humanoid with scales like reptiles, entry points to absorb energy. Her face was that of a man, and her body was that of a woman. Her eyes were large and wide, her fingernails long and sharp, her ears were pointy like an elf, and large, black, feathery wings grew out of her back, which matched her black hair.

Light emanated from her, shining a bright blue glow. Paschar is the angel of vision. In her righteous state, she was responsible for guarding the veil between the physical world and the heavens, consciousness and unconsciousness, awareness, and illusion. She once saw the beauty of visions from the Almighty and projected these into human consciousness. Now, she was limited, capable only of seeing physical beauty, extracting energy from mortal man, and projecting illusions.

Her authority was stripped from the heavens and placed on that of the Earth. Paschar growled in anger and frustration at her circumstance. She reigned over the creatures before her as if she could control them, seducing them with what she *used* to be. The truth is the fall had weakened her, weakened them, and now there was no chance at redemption. The Almighty had forsaken them, cast them aside for pieces of rotting flesh. How dare he release his own from eternal glory and offer it to the beast that is man? The pupils in Paschar's eyes widened, and the blue rays grew brighter.

"Remember who you are," she growled. The creatures responded by screeching and shooting fire from their nostrils.

When Paschar snapped her fingers, the creatures turned back into beautiful women, the customers were no longer frozen, and Pas had her African skin back. The clinging sound of new patrons entering the restaurant sounded, and three black men walked in, their eyes already on their table. The five women smiled, just as beautiful as they were before, and Paschar smoothed out the wrinkles in her skirt, licking her lips. She didn't even have to turn around. She saw them first, and her stomach growled. It was feeding time.

CHAPTER EIGHT

Erica: You need to come in.

Tina: I know. I'm sorry. I will.

Erica: I'm serious T. Don't miss another session or I'll have to report your ass :-/

Tina: Lol. I won't. ☺

Although she had added a smiley face and "Lol," to Erica's text message, Tina rolled her eyes in real life. Erica was cool, but she was still a therapist, and Tina was still her client. One more reminder text, call, and email, and Tina was going to scream. Before Az showed up again, she never missed a session, but that was before she knew what she knew. And even though Erica was the most down-to-Earth, most friendly homegirl-type therapist she could have asked for, she still couldn't tell her *everything*.

Tina rubbed her temples with her thumbs. She was sitting in her car outside of the office, deciding what to do. *Maybe Erica's right. This is crazy. I need to just go home*. Fred had turned up nothing on Jason anyway. She couldn't help him if she wanted to. The sound of a new message appeared. *Damn Erica*.

Janiyah: Miss Bernice wanted me to ask if you were on your way.

Tina sighed in relief.

Tina: On my way now ☺

Janiyah: K ☺

"I know where he is."

Tina dropped the phone and jumped at the sound of Az's voice. He had made his body smaller and was sitting in the back seat of her car.

"Don't do that!" She shook her head.

"I'm sorry."

"You always say sorry and then you keep doing it."

"I know where he is. You can stop him."

"Why me? Why can't you just let me live my life?"

“I told you. Ronnie opened a door when he agreed to work for Big Sam.”

“What’s she got to do with it? Besides, Ronnie’s dead, as you already know,” Tina sighed. To be an angel, he sure was simple-minded.

“Ronnie may be dead, but a door is still open. You are still connected. This is your mission. It’s what The Power wants. It will help you to develop your light.”

Tina shook her head, “Whatever.”

“He’s visiting his parents in Oak Park. From there, he will head to a friend’s house, but they are not there.”

“That’s a good thing, right?”

“No.”

“Oh. Okay,” Tina rolled her eyes at Az through the rearview mirror. He ignored her human emotions.

“It is too late for his friends, but you can save him if you hurry. He is wrapping up now. I can show you the way.”

“Okay, but how am I supposed to stop him?”

“You will figure it out.”

“You know it’s amusing to me how you this big bad protective angel, but you can never tell me exactly what it is I am supposed to do.”

"It would not help you to develop your light. I can show you the way, but you have to walk through the door. It must be your own choice."

"What's all this light talk? *Developing my light*. What does that even mean?"

Az vanished, leaving an address on Tina's GPS to lead her to Jason's parents' house. But the address vanished, and a map of the city with red lines appeared.

"What the…?"

Tina tapped the GPS device, trying to get it to go back to the address.

"It is too late for that," said the GPS lady's voice, "He has already gone. Follow the instructions on your screen. Hurry. There is not much time. Turn left on Columbia Boulevard."

Tina shook her head, knowing the voice was really Az. She picked up the phone.

Tina: Not gonna make it in time for dinner. Tell Miss Bernice I'll pay extra. See you in a bit.

Amy stood by the window of her office and shook her head. Tina had left fifteen minutes ago but was still sitting outside in the car, her hands moving around.

"Hey Fred?"

Frederick packed up his things to go. It was the end of the day, and the rest of the staff had already left.

"Come over here a sec."

Fred walked to the window and stood next to Amy. Both peered out the window through the blinds.

"What's she doing?" asked Amy, frowning.

Fred watched in surprise as Tina waved her hands and appeared to be talking.

"Is she on the phone?"

Amy turned to face Fred.

"Do you see a phone? She's talking to herself, again!"

Fred sighed. He didn't want to believe it was true. Maybe it was too early for her to be back. Amy turned around to the window.

"Told you," she said, her arms folded.

Fred walked away from the window and pulled his cell from his pocket. He didn't care for Amy too much, but damn it, if she wasn't right. He put the phone up to his ear as it rang, shaking his head at Amy still peaking through the window. She was so nosy. He turned his back, grabbed his belongings, and headed for the door as the line picked up.

"Hey Erica. It's me. You got some time? There's something I think you should know."

CHAPTER NINE

Jason kissed Amarie on the cheek.

"Be good," he commanded.

"Alright Ma, I'm out," he said, hugging his mother. Dad had already said his goodbyes and was at the races by now. Jason shook his head. *That man and the dog track*. He had given him some good advice, though. Mainly, he shouldn't trust that woman and he was stupid for even going over there. He was sure to give the lecture on "a woman's ways." Jason's dad thought women were sneaky and often did more dirt than men. Every woman except his wife that was.

"She probably tried to hoodoo yo ass. I'd stay away from her," Dad had said. Jason laughed at the thought. The old man had his way of warning you. Jason wasn't sure what it was, but he was glad he left when he did. Besides, it wasn't like he was going to see her again anyway.

Jason entered his car, honked his horn, and drove down the street. He was driving for a while when he came to a stoplight.

Jason picked up his cell and typed.

"See what the fellas doing."

A horn went off behind him.

"Move it buddy!" someone yelled.

"Aiight, aiight," he said, noticing the light was green.

Jason knew he shouldn't try to text while driving, but he did it anyway, and he figured everyone did. Jason had confidence that he was careful, casting his eyes on the road and back down to the phone. Jason never missed a beat. *I'm good at this,* he thought as he put the finishing touches on his text. The sound of a screeching car, honking horns, and the smell of rubber tires sounded around him as his car jolted forward, knocking the phone out of his hand.

"Oh shit!" he pulled over.

The cars around him pulled away, slowing down to five miles per hour to see the damage. Jason got out of the car as another car pulled up behind him.

"Damn," he said at the dent in the back as the driver of the other car parked behind him. He glanced up. It was a woman. *Figures*. In Jason's mind, women couldn't drive. It was what he observed from women he knew and women he dated.

He loved his mom, but he didn't think she knew how to drive either.

The woman stepped out of her car wearing black, fitted pants, a white blouse, and high-heeled shoes. Her hair was pinned up on the top of her head, and her earrings were pearl studs. Those pants filled out in the back. Jason found himself staring.

"I'm so sorry. I don't know what happened," complained the woman.

You slammed into my shit is what happened.

"It's not too bad," he lied, exhaling, hands in his pockets. He noticed the woman was staring at the car with a blank facial expression. She looked like she didn't know what to do. He took his hand out of his pocket and held it out for her.

"I'm Jason."

The woman pulled her eyes away from the car, perked up and took his extended hand.

"Oh, sorry. I don't know where my mind is these days. Tina. Nice to meet you."

Her hands were soft and melted into his palm like butter. *This is not the time*, Jason said to his hardening manhood. Just her hands alone had turned him on. This was different. But after what had happened with that other woman, he had to keep it together. She would probably try to *hoodoo* him, too. He quickly let her hand go.

"Umm." Tina dug into her purse and retrieved a card. "I guess we can exchange insurance cards until the cops get here."

"Yeah, mine is in the car. I'll get it for you." Jason turned away to retrieve his information. While getting it out of the glovebox, he noticed the woman had also returned to her car. She appeared to be shaking her head in frustration. Jason withdrew from the vehicle and walked up to her car. She was talking into her GPS. He frowned. That was kind of weird. He didn't think they worked that way. Maybe hers was broken. *Or maybe she was one of those hoodoo women.*

"Those things are the worst," he said, and Tina jumped at his voice.

"Didn't mean to scare you. Are you alright?"

Tina threw the GPS in the back seat and straightened up.

"Yeah, I'm sorry again. This is a mess."

"It's okay, really. Here's my card. Police should be here any minute now. I'm supposed to meet up with some friends. I wish they would hurry up."

Tina took Jason's card and gave him hers.

"I know right?"

Jason and Tina engaged in small talk as time passed, and Jason became more and more frustrated. It had been almost thirty minutes and no sign of the cops. Jason looked at his phone.

"Man, where the hell they at?" At his complaint, the red and blue lights appeared in the distance.

"About damn time."

Tina bit her lip. "Listen, this is my fault. I'm sorry again. I didn't mean to make you miss your friends."

Damn would she stop apologizing.

"It's all good. Do me a favor, though?"

"Yes, anything."

"Stop apologizing!" he laughed.

Damn she cute.

"Okay, I hear you. I'll stop apologizing," she smiled.

***

Tina's hands wouldn't stop shaking. She hoped Jason didn't hear her talking to Az through the GPS. He was a pain in her butt.

"Let me make it up to you," she said.

Jason smirked and Tina's heart fluttered.

"Are you asking me out?" he asked, eyebrow raised, dimple piercing his cheeks.

"I guess I am."

Jason rubbed his hands together. "Wow. I never had a girl ask me on a date before."

Tina hit his arm, "That's right because I'm a woman."

Jason stepped back, holding his chest, "Dang woman, is that how you treat all your dates? You violent."

They laughed.

"I guess everything is okay here?"

Tina and Jason looked at each other and then back to the officer. They didn't even see him walk up. He held a pen and small notepad in his hands.

"Yeah, we good," said Jason, cutting his eyes at Tina.

"Who hit who?" The officer sounded irritated.

"She hit me."

"Give a sista up just like that, huh?"

"You did hit me though. Twice," he said rubbing his arm.

Tina shook her head and Jason winked.

The cop cleared his throat and Jason pulled his attention away from Tina.

Turn right on green.

Tina's nerves returned. *Uh-oh. Az.*

While Jason signed papers, she took the time to return to the car and reach for the device in the back seat.

"I knew you would find a way," sounded the GPS. Hitting his car was brilliant," said the GPS lady.

Tina relaxed. "Yeah, well, just wait until he finds out I did it on purpose and that our meeting was no accident. He'll hate me forever."

She stole a glance at Jason from the window of her car. He looked up at her and smiled. She smiled back, halfheartedly. Chicago police were slow, especially when it came to minorities. Her little trick should keep him away just long enough to keep him from meeting up with those friends Az already said were doomed. Tina sighed. She had saved the man. Mission accomplished. Her work here was done.

Or so she thought.

CHAPTER TEN

Big Steve felt the phone vibrate in his jeans as they entered El Che Steakhouse and Bar, but he ignored it. This was like one of those movies where someone sees a white light during a near-death experience, but this light was blue.

"Hey, fam! Ya'll see that?"

Big Steve tapped his friends, Chris and Marquise, as they made it to their table on the other side of the restaurant.

"Damn," said Marquise.

The men sat down at the table.

"Look like it's our lucky day fellas," said Chris.

Steve pointed to the table in the distance, "Look at they eyes though."

"I ain't fucking her eyes," Chris laughed.

"I'm serious, though. Ya'll don't think that's weird?"

Marquise shrugged, "You never heard of contacts bro?"

"I ain't never seen contacts that bright."

The waitress approached the table as the men stared at the booth across the room with the beautiful blue-eyed women.

"What can I get you gentlemen?"

The men were silent, staring at the other table. The waitress waved her hand.

"Hello?" she rolled her eyes.

"Uh yeah, water," said Chris."

The waitress put her hands on her hips, looked over at the other table and then back to the men. She thought it was weird they were staring at an empty booth, but she had worked all day and didn't have time to think about what they were up to. She just hoped it wasn't running off on the bill.

"Everybody want water?"

"Yep," said Marquise, still staring across the room.

"Let me get a shot of Crown, no ice," said Steve.

The waitress wrote down the order, rolled her eyes again and walked off.

Chris got up from the table.

"Aye," said Steve. "What you doing?"

"Imma go talk to her."

"What?"

"I ain't about to sit here with my tongue out like you niggas. I got my eye on that Japanese one. I love when they little like that."

The men laughed, and the women across the room all turned to look at them, their crystal blue eyes piercing.

It was like a lucid dream. Either this wasn't happening, or they were three of the luckiest men on Earth. Time seemed to stop as the women looked deeply into their eyes from across the room.

"Maybe I should just sit here a minute," said Chris, unable to take his eyes off the Japanese one. He didn't know if she was that fine or if he actually couldn't look away.

In seconds, the women appeared right in front of them, their bodies bursting out of their clothing. Steve didn't know how they had made it over to their table so quickly or how the thickest, darkest, sexiest one found her way onto his lap, his chin in her hands, her eyes locked on his. He wiped his brow. It had suddenly gotten hot.

***

Paschar turned around, slowly, careful to pay attention to every inch of her body. As she locked eyes with the biggest man at the table, her girls followed suit, rays of blue light shooting like lasers into the men's eyes. They had frozen time and within seconds had glided over to the table. It didn't matter that there were six of them and three of the men. Men who thought they were getting orgies were the easiest victims.

Paschar sat her booty on top of the man's lap, strategically placing it on the part of his jeans where his penis was rock hard. Their lips met, and she kissed him deeply, forcefully. She enjoyed the kissing, their tongues lapping onto the other, the fresh taste of his scent. She could taste his essence, his past, and his present. Everything that led him to this place was on her tongue. Everyone in the restaurant disappeared, and it was just her and him.

She inhaled, and with it, sucked the oxygen out of his lungs, gradually suffocating him. Big Steve's eyes bulged surprise, and his erect penis was now limp at the door of death. He couldn't breathe. He knew there was something strange about these women, but it was too late. She had latched onto his mouth and wouldn't let go. He pushed his 200-pound frame against her body, but she was like concrete. How in the hell was she stronger than he was? The color drained from his face as he pushed, but the woman didn't move. Steve's head got smaller as his body shrunk; his skin clung to his bones. The same was happening to his friends. Their clothing was getting bigger and baggy as the women sucked the energy from their bodies. Paschar kept her lips locked on Steve's and sucked until he was a hollow corpse before her.

She stood and searched the man's pockets for the device that kept vibrating. She touched the screen. She learned how to operate cell phones years ago. It was strange how addicted the humans were to it, but she had to respect Hephaestus's work, god of technology. He was getting his just as she had just gotten hers. She read the letters on the screen.

Jason: Aye, I'm on my way, where ya'll at?

Jason: Steve…

Jason: Aye, Steve where ya'll at?

Jason: Hey man I'm not gonna be able to make it, somebody hit my shit, call me.

Jason: Hey man, sorry I missed ya'll earlier. We got it taken care of. Tried calling. Hit me back. Peace.

Paschar smiled, wiping the sides of her mouth with a finger as Steve's energy pulsated throughout her body. The girls had finished their meals as well. She slipped the phone into her purse, and the women vanished, leaving three corpses at the table.

CHAPTER ELEVEN

Tina closed the door to her supervisor's office behind her. She wasn't sure why Juan wanted to see her, and she was even more suprised to see Fred sitting in one of the chairs in front of his desk. Amy stood next to Juan, who held a large manilla envelope. Tina folded her arms.

"What's up?"

Juan cleared his throat, rubbed his goatee, and picked up the envelope. He had come to America with his parents at just three years old and had worked hard to become one of the youngest Cuban supervisors in their unit. When teased about his common name, he'd always give a little history lesson. "Juan is the Spanish version of John and is tied with Juan Almeida Bosque, the Cuban revolutionary. It means God's gracious gift." People typically left him alone after that, not wanting to hear any more. When it came to his Cuban heritage, Juan was long-winded and could talk you to death, resurrect you, and kill you again. The only thing he was more passionate about was his job, and his co-workers always teased him about taking it too seriously. Juan and Tina typically got along and had little friction, but something was off about the room's energy. But then again, Amy was there. Tina was sure it could have just been her.

"Have a seat."

Tina looked from Juan to Fred to Amy. Fred played with his hands and Amy looked away. *Something was definitely up.*

"I'll stand."

"Please, sit."

Tina sighed and sat in the chair. Juan's office was one of the most comfortable in the building. The chairs were plush, and he stoked the bookshelves with the best literature. Juan's collection was next level. Every book you can imagine was on his shelf, from the classics to new releases, and Juan didn't discriminate, which made it fascinating. Tina paused to examine her surroundings, thinking of all the times they used to hide out in this office drinking whiskey and laughing back when he was a new detective. She even spent a night here one time when she was too wasted to drive home. It was that cozy, but now, Tina didn't feel comfortable. The room's energy was stale, the bookshelves could have been a wall closing her in, and the chair may as well have been made of concrete.

"What is this about?" she whispered to Fred. But he just shrugged and looked forward. Something about his posture was stiff and his eyes had that faraway look to it, almost robotic.

"Fred?"

Tina shook Fred's arm and he snapped out of his trance. He really needed to see someone about that daze. She looked around the room.

"What's going on?"

Juan opened the envelope and removed three photos, spreading them faced down on the desk. Tina moved her chair closer to get a better look.

"What's this?"

Juan responded by turning the pictures over, one at a time and Amy looked away.

"I can't."

Tina raised a brow in Amy's direction and twisted her lips. *Ole dramatic ass.* But when Tina looked down, she could see why Amy looked away. The images were disturbing. Tina's hand rushed to her mouth.

"Oh my God."

Three lean bodies in baggy clothing lay at a table, their eyeballs protruding from their sockets. It looked like all the fluid had been sucked out of them, and all that was left was skin and bones in oversized clothes.

Amy turned away from the office window and back toward the table, shaking her head.

“This is the El Che Steakhouse and Bar on Washington Boulevard,” said Juan. “The men were found by the waitress assigned to their table. She said she had taken the men’s orders and walked away from the table. She said as she was carrying the drinks back, she heard screams. She returned to the table and found them like this. The waitress herself screamed, dropped the glasses, and ran out of the restaurant with the other patrons. The owner called 911.

“My goodness.”

It would take a long time for her to get those images out of her head now.

“But that’s not even the weird part,” continued Juan. “This happened in broad daylight during normal business hours, but there are no witnesses to the actual murder if we can even call it murder. Customers say they didn’t see anything. Everyone remembers seeing the men enter the restaurant and sit down. They even remember seeing the waitress take the order, but that’s all. They say they looked like normal, black men coming in to eat like the rest of them. One of them was even big-boned, you know, heavyset.”

Amy chuckled. People said *big boned* to keep from saying fat, and she knew Juan was extra sensitive around Fred, who was a bit on the heavy side himself. *He was fat. Say that*, she thought.

"But no one saw them suffering in any way."

"That's impossible. Someone had to see something," Tina said touching each of the pictures.

Juan took a deep breath and Amy looked down at her feet.

Why are they acting like they were just caught kissing and I'm the mama?

"Come on ya'll. What's going on? Ya'll know you can keep it real with me. I don't like all this beating around the bush stuff."

"I looked into Jason like you asked me to," said Fred.

So, you do remember how to talk.

"I didn't find anything, as you know."

The mention of Jason's name made Tina's heart beat fast.

"I know," she said annoyed. They had already been over this.

"I did find he's connected to these men though. Did you know that?"

Tina tilted her head and frowned.

"Of course, I didn't know."

Fred sat up in his seat and leaned forward.

"Here's what I don't get. You ask me to look into a man and not even two days later that man's friends are dead?"

"Wait, you're not saying I had anything to do with this?"

Fred sat back. "No, of course not."

Tina stood. "Then what *are* you saying?"

"T, girl calm down."

Tina looked at Amy. "Don't tell me to calm down like you ain't just hear him passively accuse me of having prior knowledge of these men's murders. What are you doing here, anyway? This isn't your case."

Juan held up a hand, "We don't know if it's a murder."

"I'm here because Mr. Emerson asked me to be here, okay?"

Tina turned her attention back to Fred, torturing him with her eyes.

"Listen Tina, you've been through a lot and…" began Juan but Tina held up a hand.

"Don't patronize me…"

"We just think you need a break is all."

"What?"

Juan pressed a button on the office phone and Tina stepped back at the voice coming through the speaker.

"You haven't been to any sessions; you barely answer my calls. We're worried about you T."

Tina shook her head, trying to hold the anger back. It was Erica.

"You were listening the entire time? What is this, an intervention?"

"Can you tell us why you've been talking to yourself?" asked Amy.

"I don't owe any of you an explanation."

Juan cleared his throat. "You kinda do."

"This is bullshit."

"Answer her question Tina," said Fred. "What's going on with you?"

Tina thought back to a bathroom conversation with Az. Amy caught her talking with him there, but she felt she explained that away. She knew it would come back to haunt her.

"I was just using the bathroom. Give me a break."

"No," said Fred. "There's another time. You were sitting in the car outside of the office, moving your hands and I don't know if you were praying or…"

Tina waved. "Oh, come on. What I do in *my* car is *my* business."

"I saw it with my own eyes, T," chimed Amy. "You were sitting there talking to yourself. That's twice now."

"And," added Erica, "you haven't been to a session in like two weeks, so I can't even vouch for where your head is right now."

"What's the plan? Huh? You gonna fire me? Just come out and say what it is you brought me here to say."

"How do you know Jason?" asked Juan.

"You told me before you think he may be connected," said Fred pointing to the photographs "And now we see that he *is* connected. How did you know this?"

"First don't say *know this* like I knew three black men were going to die yesterday!"

"Yes, but you know what I'm talking about Tina. How did you know about Jason in the first place?"

She felt convicted and forced the lump of tears back down her throat. It did sound suspicious, but Tina couldn't tell them about Az. She already told Erica about seeing aliens, and she was standing against her, which meant she never believed her in the first place. Tina thought she believed her. Erica spoke to her as if she did and even told Tina to get more information on the humans involved. *So, all that talk about 'see who are all connected' was some bullshit.* Tina felt like an idiot. Erica must have heard crazy stories like hers all the time and was probably entertaining her. She turned away from Fred and faced Juan.

"I had a hunch."

"That's *some* hunch T. Come on," said Fred.

"I don't think I was talking to you."

Fred was starting to piss her off. He held up his hands.

"I'm just trying to help. I am here for you. You know that."

"Hey Erica? I'll be in touch," said Juan, hanging up the phone. He leaned back into his chair and twirled a pen around his fingers.

"Take some time off."

"Time off meaning what? Are you firing me?"

"Tina, you know I wouldn't do that. Paid time off. Get your head in the game."

Tina rolled her eyes and walked out of the office.

Amy looked at Fred. "Well. That went well."

"I don't know what's gotten into her. Ever since her nephew died, she hasn't been the same."

Juan looked down at the photos and shook his head. He hated to suspect Tina of anything. They were cool but that was *some* hunch.

"Keep an eye on her," he said, his eyes still on the photographs. "I think she's involved. I wanna know how, and I wanna know why."

CHAPTER TWELVE

Sweat pooled along Jason's forehead, poured down his face, and dripped from his body. Shirtless, he furiously attacked the bag, beating it with all the anger inside of him. Word on the street was that Big Steve, Marquise, and Chris were murdered at El Che the other day. Not only was this unexpected, but it reminded him of how close he had come to his own death. He was supposed to meet with them that night. If it weren't for that car accident, he would be dead too. *Damn*, he thought of Tina. *That woman saved my life.* She still had not given him a definite date for when he could take her out, but he'd have to treat her to something special. He was eternally grateful, even if also sad. Never could he have imagined in just one day, he would lose all his friends. He didn't understand how no one had seen anything when it happened in broad daylight in front of a room full of people. It was also reported that Steve's phone was missing, which would explain why he didn't answer his texts. Jason didn't believe the cops and detectives and assumed they were not doing their job as usual to solve his friend's case. *Was it because they were all black men?* There was no way no one knew anything. There was no way no one saw anything, and now he had to think about organizing a fundraiser to raise the money to bury his friends.

"Ah!" Jason yelled out loud in frustration.

"Everything gonna be alright man," said Eddie, Jason's workout partner. "Somebody gonna find out something."

Jason sat down on a bench and wiped his head and chest with a towel. "It's just not making sense. How the hell three men die in your establishment in broad damn daylight, and nobody see nothing? Somebody lying."

"I agree with that bro, for real," said Eddie punching a bag.

"They saying it might be drug related."

"What?"

"Yeah man, talking about they found cocaine in they system."

"What?" Eddie said again.

"And you know my brothers didn't smoke. We may have hit some weed or something but not that other shit."

"I know," agreed Eddie. That's not how Jason rolled. He didn't get high, and he didn't hang with people who got high.

Jay wasn't perfect, but Eddie knew he wouldn't hang around no scrubs.

Jason's cell rang and he stared at the screen in disbelief.

"What the…?"

Eddie stopped punching the bag and Jason showed him the screen.

"Steve?"

Jason pulled the phone back. "What I say about people playing games?"

"That's some spooky shit," said Eddie.

Silence filled the room as the phone went silent and then started vibrating again.

Eddie tilted his head in thought. "Didn't they say Big Steve's phone was missing? Yo, answer that!"

"Hello?"

Eddie thought he would stop breathing as they listened on speakerphone.

"Hello?"

Jason hung up and grabbed his shirt off the bench, pulling it over his head. "Aye, man, I'm out. Gotta find out what the hell is going on here."

"Take care of your business, man."

The men hugged, fist bumped, and Jason was out the door. Eddie returned to punching the bag in front of him.

***

Paschar exhaled and hung up. Jason's soul was something she craved. His friends were okay, but their energy wasn't as potent as his. She thought back on the day of their deaths, remembering how she had to empty them to hit the spot. It was like being thirsty and drinking water that never quite quench the thirst. To humans it seemed as if they could stop time, but that was beyond their power. They could only slow things down so much that time seemed to stop. Things were still moving, just much slower. Paschar laughed. The waitress was no threat. She had walked past the men's table three times while they suffered but didn't see them. Slowing time made Paschar and her legion invisible and their work easier. She knew the men would also be invisible to humans once they had attached themselves. To the mortals, it would be as if nothing had happened, the table empty of people until she left their corpses to rot.

CHAPTER THIRTEEN

Jason's head pounded as he drove to the nearest police station. Thankfully, Amarie was still with his parents. He had not gone back to get her since the news came. They understood and offered to give him as much time as he needed. "Just remember this is *your* daughter," his dad cautioned. Jason cursed under his breath at the Chicago traffic and hoped the cops could trace the call back to the killer.

Jason almost missed the station, made a u-turn, and barely parked his car when he jumped out of it and ran into the building.

"I need to speak to someone," he said to the receptionist, a white woman with brown freckles and glasses that hung off the tip of her nose. She frowned at the sweaty-faced, out-of-breath man with the wet t-shirt and grabbed a sticky note.

"About?"

"I got some information about the El Che Steakhouse murders."

The woman removed her glasses and raised a brow.

"What kind of information?"

***

"What am I supposed to do then, Az? They are getting suspicious. You know they suspended a bitch."

Tina smiled pretentiously at the mother and child that walked by, adjusting her earbuds and holding her mobile device. Az was sitting next to her on the park bench, and his large body towered over her. Tina was going to be smart this time. Since no one else could see him, she would have her earbuds in and her mobile in plain sight each time she spoke with Az. She even put the phone to her ear now and again. It would be obvious she's *on the phone* from now on.

"Good. Now you can focus on saving Jason."

"What are you talking about? You told me to stop him from meeting his friends. I did that."

"Yes. You did very well with the car accident, but Jason is still in danger."

Tina shook her head. "This shit is for the birds. Maybe I should just tell him about you."

"Be careful with that. Paschar was a leader for a reason. You have to expect her to be ten steps ahead of you. Assume she already knows about you."

"My mama said don't make assumptions 'cause you make a ass out of me and you."

"Assume this time."

"It was a joke."

"I see."

"Sheesh. Lighten up. Angels don't laugh?"

"Trust no one," said Az, vanishing.

Tina typed into her phone.

Tina: Hey. It's Tina. Can I meet you somewhere?

***

Juan typed into his computer and scribbled words onto a notepad. They were still investigating the death of Byron Fisher, and now three more men had died. They were being slaughtered with paperwork and follow-ups.

"Mr. Emerson? You have a visitor."

Juan sighed and kept typing.

"Mr. Emerson?"

"One moment, Kathy," he said, finishing the last of the sentence his secretary had interrupted. "Do you think you can handle that for me? We're swamped in here today."

"He says he's got information on the Steakhouse murders. Says he has an appointment?"

Juan stopped typing and looked up. He hated how Kathy said everything like it ended in a question. He shook his head at the minor distraction.

"We don't know if it's murder. Send him in."

"Good afternoon. I'm Detective Emerson. Please, have a seat."

He watched as the man sat and looked around the room. Juan smiled. That was the usual response to his office.

"What can I do for you? I hear you have information on the Steakhouse case?"

The man pulled out a cell phone and started scrolling.

"I need ya'll to track this number." He put the phone down on the desk.

"That number belongs to Steve. Steve is my friend," the man sniffed. "*Was* my friend. My *best* friend."

"Okay," said Juan picking up the phone. He recalled Steve being one of the names of the victims. "And by Steve, you mean Steve Richardson?"

A tear escaped the man's eye, but he wiped it away quickly.

"Yes. Steve Richardson, Chris Washington, and Marquis Johnson. Those were my friends, and I believe whoever killed them called me from that number. Why? I don't know. That's why I'm here, but I know I got a call from that number and that's Steve's number, and I don't know what's going on, but I need someone to explain to me why a dead man is calling my phone."

Juan reached for a sticky note and wrote the number down. He gave the phone back to Jason and leaned back in his seat.

"Did you say these were your friends?"

"Yeah man, so what ya'll gonna do? Can't you put some tracking on that or something?"

Juan typed into the computer. "I'm sorry. I never got your name."

"Jason."

Juan nodded. *So, this is Jason.*

"What?"

Juan cleared his throat. He hadn't meant to stare. "I'm sorry, this is just the first real lead in this case."

Juan leaned back in his chair. This could be a real opportunity for them. Tina's suspension can prove more valuable than they had anticipated. She needed to be out of the picture for what he had in mind.

Jason's phone vibrated, and he looked down at it and typed.

"Look, I gotta go. Ya'll gonna help me solve my brother's murder or what?"

"First, it's not technically a murder. There is no proof that anyone killed these men. No witnesses and no weapon. Right now, it's looking like a freak accident."

Jason waved his hand, "That's bullshit."

"It's called asphyxiam," said Juan. "It's what happens when your body doesn't get enough oxygen to keep you from passing out. When you breathe normally, first, you take in oxygen. Your lungs send that oxygen into your blood, which carries it to your tissues. Then your cells use it to make energy. Any interruption to the process of breathing in oxygen and breathing out carbon dioxide can make you pass out or lose your life."

"What's your point?"

"The point is it looks as if the men suffocated. On what we don't know."

Jason laughed, "So you are telling me that three grown men suffocated. All three of them."

"Look, the investigation is still ongoing. I am not even supposed to be having this conversation with you. There is only one witness, and she said the men hadn't ordered any food yet, just drinks. They were too focused on some women at another table."

Jason jumped up.

“Whoa, women? What women? Write that shit down!”

Juan held up a hand, “Except, the waitress didn’t see anyone.”

“If my man’s nem said they saw women, they saw women. How ya’ll gonna just leave that out?”

“No one’s leaving anything out, but we cannot accept the testimony of dead men. The waitress is our only witness. She said the men claimed to be looking at some women at another table, but she didn’t see anything when she looked. She thought they were trying to run out on the bill.”

“Man, her ass is lying!”

“As you can see, I have a lot of work to do.”

Jason stormed out of the door.

CHAPTER FOURTEEN

"Good afternoon! What can I get you?"

Pas smiled, feeling giddy and youthful in her skin. She had transformed into the body of a fifteen-year-old Ethiopian girl. As Tina gave her order, Paschar smiled. They had finally met.

"Caramel macchiato, please."

"Coming right up!"

Tina smiled, and Pas studied her energy as she downloaded the skill to make the drink. As she prepared it, she saw into Tina's future. She saw her and Jason speaking with Az and their plan to destroy the operation at Altgeld. That was Big Sam's territory, now under the leadership of Renita and Scar and the authority of her legion sister, Hitomi.

Pas watched as Tina tugged at her collar, her temperature rising. Paschar wanted so much to dig. To reach into the depths of Tina's soul and destroy everything she'd ever loved. If she wanted, she could download everything about her in a manner of seconds and leave her empty on the Starbucks floor.

"Here you go!"

She watched as Tina took the drink and watched her sit at the table in the corner, her back to the wall. Tina caught her staring and waved. Pas waved back, smiling.

But not now. She couldn't dig. Tina was the key to how she'd get close to Jason again, and she was no use to her dead.

***

The Starbucks was buzzing with customers, as usual, the smell of their signature blend addicting everyone's nostrils. Writers sat with their laptops open, and couples laughed in hushed tones over coffee. Tina smiled. *Could that be us? Could we be a couple?* She dismissed the thought just as quickly as she considered it. She had too much on her plate to think about a relationship.

"Good afternoon! What can I get for you?"

Tina smiled at the young girl behind the counter. She was a pretty girl and had to be no older than sixteen. Tina ordered her coffee and carried it over to a table in the corner of the room.

She liked to sit with her back to the wall so she could see every angle. She smiled as the girl waved at her. *So sweet.*

Jason walked through the door and looked around. Tina held up her hand and waved, smiling. He smiled back and walked toward her.

"Look, T, there's something I gotta tell you."

Tina's heart raced and she played with her hands. If he said something sexy like he was falling for her she would never gather the courage to tell him the truth.

"Let me go first. Please."

"I really think I need to tell you first."

"No," said Tina. "I texted you so I'm calling it."

Jason laughed. "Okay."

"This is going to sound crazy…"

"Uh-oh, don't tell me you got some crazy baby daddy."

"That depends. Is your baby mama crazy?"

The two laughed. Tina knew about Amarie. Jason had told her the first day they met, right after the police left the day of the accident, and they exchanged numbers. She could tell he loved his daughter. He had explained that he wanted to be straight up.

"I see things."

Jason frowned.

"Well, not things, really. People."

"You see dead people?"

"I'm trying to be serious!"

"Then don't try. Do it."

"Smart ass."

Jason laughed, "You're the one seeing people."

"Well, not people. More like, angels."

"Oh, so you one of those super sensitive spiritual people, huh?"

"I guess you can say that."

Jason nodded, and Tina relaxed a little. He didn't seem turned off. Az said there was still a door open, a connection to Big Sam's people attracting Paschar's legion to her family. Her secret had to be the door, which meant she had to come clean.

"His name is Azbuga and he knows about your friends' murders. He can help you," Tina blurted out.

"What are you talking about?"

Tina fidgeted. Jason didn't look impressed.

"Az, the angel."

Jason sat back in his chair and folded his arms.

"You're serious."

"As a heart attack."

Jason rubbed his hands together. “Come on now.”

“Wait, just let me finish. Az can help us. He knows the women who killed your friends and…”

Jason put up his hand, “How do you know about the women?”

Tina frowned, “How do *you* know about the women?”

CHAPTER FIFTEEN

Juan sat upright in his office chair, his face grave. Officer Parks and Officer Jones, detectives who were part of the Ja'mella case, stood on the side of him, looking down at the computer. Jones folded his arms and scratched his bald head. Parks stood five inches shorter than him, her gray dreadlocks wrapped around her head in a sloppy bun. She shook her head. Parks knew Tina from the Ja'mella case and still considered her a friend.

"She's a little out there, but what do we *really* have on her?"

There was silence as the detectives sat in thought.

"Exactly," continued Parks, "We have nothing concrete that connects her to the murders."

"For the last time, we do not know if it was a murder."

Parks suppressed a laugh. Juan took his job way too serious.

"And," he continued. "We *do* know that she knew about Jason."

Parks shrugged, "That proves nothing."

"She might not be involved, but she knows something."

The door to Juan's office opened, and Fred's face peeked in.

"Hey."

Juan closed his laptop. He forgot he called Fred in for a meeting. He was promoting him as an informant to spy on Tina. Now that they knew Jason was involved, he would spy on them both.

"Yes, come on in."

Fred opened the door wider and entered the office.

"Detectives," he said, nodding his head at Officer Carl Jones and Rosalee Parks. Concern flashed across Fred's face, and his eyebrows buried deep into his forehead. He sure hoped he wasn't being fired.

"What's this about?"

Tina and Jason exited Starbucks and sat in her car.

"How long have you known about the women?"

"Only since yesterday. I got a call from Big Steve's phone. The one they said was missing. That's why I went to the station. I'm not even supposed to be telling you this."

"It's okay. Mr. Emerson's my boss."

"What?"

Tina sighed and looked out of the window.

"Yep. Juan Emerson."

Jason frowned, "Wait. You're a detective?"

Tina turned to face Jason.

"There is something else I have to tell you. Don't get mad, but I hit you on purpose. The car accident. It was Az and me."

"Who the hell is Az?"

"I already told you."

Jason rubbed his temples. He finally found someone he liked, and she was weird.

"He's a Watcher Archangel. He looks like a really tall Hispanic guy, but he's not really Hispanic because angels don't have a race like us. He sounds white, though," Tina chuckled.

Jason spoke with his hands, "I don't see anything funny about this. Do you hear yourself?"

"I'm telling you the truth."

There was silence. Mr. Emerson was right. He had briefed him on the death of Ronnie and how Tina hadn't been the same since. According to Juan, they had caught her talking to herself. He thought they were reaching with that. People grieve differently, so no process is wrong. But now, with all this angel talk, it had him thinking, maybe they were right. She might not have been one of those hoodoo women, but he couldn't take any chances.

"Anyway. We caused the accident because we had to save you. Or else you would be dead, too."

Her last comment pissed him off.

"You a damn detective this whole time, but you can't give me any information about what happened to my friends. At least Mr. Emerson told me something that halfway makes sense."

"Can you just call him Juan?"

"Tina. I'm not playing games with you. What do you know about who killed my friends? Who are these women? And I don't wanna hear shit about no damn angels."

"Then you don't want the truth."

Jason's jaw clenched, and he stepped out of the vehicle.

"Going to get Amarie. When you ready to talk, you know where to find me."

CHAPTER SIXTEEN

Tina plugged her phone into the charger and changed into her pajamas. As she changed, she thought about Janiyah. They had their worst fight earlier, and Janiyah's words had pierced her to the core. It had not occurred to her that she was neglecting the children, something she promised never to do. There used to be a time when Miss Bernice was not allowed to cook for her family. Now it seemed she made dinner for them every night. Dinner was supposed to be their time together.

Tina's heart sank as she climbed into bed. Between being a fulltime mother, dating Jason, and avoiding Juan's accusation there was just too much going on, and she didn't know if she could take much more. Silently, she gave her props to the mothers pulling double duty. She was struggling and had no idea how she would balance it all. Having children was one thing and being married with children was another thing. But being a single mom to children that weren't biologically yours was a Goliath, and she was no David. She wanted to call in help, a referee, someone to lighten the burden that had become her life. It wasn't supposed to happen like this. She was supposed to marry the love of her life and have her own children. Tina cringed.

She hated to say it like that. Niyah, Mike, and KK were just as much hers as if they had come from her womb. Tina helped Keisha to raise them and became their aunt. But as much as she loved Keisha's kids, she still yearned for seeds of her own flesh. *Was this selfish?* Tina was sure that it was, but she was also sure that she was human, and the societal, biological clock ingrained in her ticked, and every time it ticked, she hurt from loss. These were supposed to be the days she and Keisha dreamed about as teens. These were those "grown-up" years where they were supposed to be gazillionaires with huge families and took trips to Dubai just because they could afford it. While Keisha successfully had her dream four, Tina wished she hadn't had any children. And while Tina graduated high school and headed to college, Keisha dropped out of school to raise Janiyah and then quickly got pregnant again. This time a boy, Tyrone, who everybody called Ronnie. She had hoped to get her GED and attend community college, but then she had Michael and soon after, Kayla. Keisha gave up hope and started giving that hope to the streets. She was hooked before Tina could walk across the stage.

Tina's phone pinged from an incoming text, interrupting her thinking.

Freddy: Hey, can we talk? I'm sorry about my behavior lately. I know Ronnie's death was hard on you. Can you meet me tomorrow?

Tina's lip curled up. Fred had been her partner for five years. He had been there for her when Ronnie died and had always been by her side. It was nice to see he had not completely lost his mind.

Tina: Sure.

Tina turned the phone off, turned over, and raised the covers over her head.

***

Fred sat deep in thought about his next move. He had to protect Tina no matter what. But then, what information could he give to Juan?

Tina waved her hand in front of her friend's face.

"Earth to Fred. You are not checking out on me again, are you?"

Fred turned to her and smiled. "Haven't I always been there for you T?"

Tina sighed and sipped her coffee, closing her eyes and letting the coolness of the wind caress her face. A dog barked, and someone's child screamed. Tina's eyes popped open and scanned the park and then back around to face Freddy. They had met here before heading to the office, so it wasn't unusual to meet so early in the morning. They did it all the time. But hindsight is twenty-twenty.

"Of course, Fred, c'mon."

"You say that, but I'm worried about you T. Seriously. What's going on?"

Tina sighed and shook her head. She could trust Fred. But she thought she could trust Jason, too, and he snapped on her. She looked at him and smiled.

"I'm okay. Really, I am."

Fred shrugged, "I'll never stop worrying about you, T, but if you say you're okay, I believe you."

Tina smiled and leaned against Fred's shoulder.

"Aww, Fred!"

They both laughed as Fred's phone rang. He held it up.

"Gotta take this. You good?"

"I'm aiight. Take your call."

"You sure?"

Tina pushed him, "Go!"

Fred stood and walked off, laughing as he put the phone to his ear. Tina smiled. At least she still had one friend.

***

Fred winced as his phone rang. He knew it was Juan wanting details, but Tina was telling him nothing. He faked a smile and walked off, leaving Tina on the park bench, sipping her coffee.

"I don't know man. She ain't budging."

"Then make her budge," said Juan's voice on the other line.

"Look, I been knowing T a long time. She trusts me. I'd like to keep it that way."

"What you'd like to keep is your job."

"Juan? Why you tripping? I can't make her tell me anything."

"You can and you will."

The line went dead, and Fred pulled the phone back and looked at it, startled by the dial tone. Everybody was acting crazy. He didn't know what to think. He was supposed to be spying on Tina, and so far, he was failing. *Something ain't right.* He had to dig deeper, and if Tina wasn't going to talk to him, someone would. Contacting her was risky, but he felt he had no choice, so he dialed the number, raising the phone to his ear.

"What's up girl? You at Altgeld tonight? Cool. Stay up. I'm coming through."

CHAPTER SEVENTEEN

Janiyah sat up on the couch, took out her flip phone and scrolled through her MySpace page.

"Tab, girl come on."

She didn't like spending too much time at Tabitha's house. She just wanted to get her money and go home. Tab lived in the Altgeld Gardens, one of the last remaining housing projects in Chicago, located on the city's far south side bordering Riverdale. The complex had undergone renovations but had continued to perpetuate the same gun violence and poverty associated with any Chicago housing complex. But that's not why Janiyah hated it. Before Tina moved them out, she had grown up in the projects, and she was pretty enough to be protected by the gang members who still lusted for her. She knew it was arrogant to think, but it was true. If the gang leaders thought you were "a dime," they showed you favor. "Redbones" were in, and everyone wanted that pretty light-skinned girl named Janiyah.

Word on the street was also that her auntie was a detective and ruled with an iron fist. While they wanted Janiyah, they also wanted to stay out of jail. And so, they watched her with lustful eyes, flirted, and hoped to navigate Tina's steel fence with the two pit bulls in front of it. Terms like, "You ready yet?" "You eighteen yet?" were common when Janiyah sashayed down the halls. Her footsteps hit the concrete with confidence, kissing the ground like she poured the cement herself or knew who did. Her laughter was a flirtatious innocence, and the way her hips danced and her booty bounced made them swear she knew what she was doing, even if she didn't. She was a goddess no one had the authority to touch, and she knew it. Janiyah walked the patio like she lived there and never had a problem, though she would never let goodie-too-shoes Tina know this is where she kicked it.

"Let me put my wig on," shouted Tabitha from the back. Janiyah smiled and shook her head.

"You got something to drink in here?"

"I think it's some Kool-Aid left."

A phone sang in the back room. Tab always had a busy line.

"Hey, stranger."

"Yeah, I'm here. What's up?"

Janiyah, smiled, shaking her head at her crazy friend. Here, she was home. But Tabitha's apartment reminded her too much of Big Sam's apartment and too much of Ronnie. He was alive then.

Big Sam was a woman, her name short for Samantha, and she was one of the biggest drug queenpins in Chicago. Her name is what made her so good because everyone assumed she was a man. Sam had men under her, though, taking orders and moving weight. She didn't have to do anything but give orders. When Janiyah met Tabitha, she had no idea she was Big Sam's cousin. They became close friends, and both got trapped. A chill ran down Janiyah's back to think of the things she used to do.

Janiyah walked over to the refrigerator and was reminded of Ronnie. She tried to warn him about Sam that day, but he was so hardheaded. She remembered him getting up from the couch and walking over to the refrigerator for some milk during their argument. That boy loved him some milk.

> You still don't get it, do you? You say you love Mama, but do you have any idea what could happen to her once our business is in the street?
>
> "There you go with that exaggerating stuff again," said Ronnie, emptying the last of the milk from the carton and putting it back.
>
> "Don't put that back. It's empty."

Janiyah laughed as she remembered, and her eyes followed the memory of her little brother walking from the refrigerator to the couch where she stood over him. It wasn't Tab's couch she was looking at now. It was Big Sam's apartment, her sofa, and Ronnie bouncing a basketball into the air, ignoring her.

"I'm the man of this house. You ain't gotta do nothing. Besides, what we got going on ain't got nothing to do with you."

"Aye Niyah," Big Sam had called. "You ready to go?"

Janiyah fought the tears rising in her throat, the sickness swirling in her stomach. She still couldn't believe she'd let Sam talk her into this. She remembered the day vividly because it was her first job. What she was doing now was easy money, but nothing compared to the first job.

"Niyah," the voice called, and Janiyah closed her eyes tight to block out the sound, tears streaming down her cheeks.

"Niyah!"

Her body stumbled backwards as Tabitha shook her.

"Girl, you alright?"

Janiyah looked around, snapping out of the memory trance and wiping her face.

"Yeah, I'm good."

Tabitha frowned. "It don't look like you good. Why you crying?"

"I'm good…for real. Let's get this over with."

Tabitha held onto Janiyah's hands.

"I know it's hard, baby, but we almost there. You only owe a few thousand now, right?"

"More like seven thousand."

"I still don't know how yo mama owed so much money. Fuck Sam have her doing?"

Janiyah shook her head.

"Well, anyway girl, you can make half of that tonight and then some. Just get it over with. Let's go make some monnay!"

The young women laughed as they left the apartment.

Greetings from the neighbors and catcalls followed them down the patio as usual. Janiyah in her snug gray Nike sweats, fitted blue tee, and white Air Force Ones and Tabitha with her jet-black wig, skin-tight blue-jeans, and black heels. Tabitha was half-Asian and half-black, and it drove the men crazy. She was a different kind of beautiful to them and not just because of her looks. Tab was straight hood and didn't give two shits about her Asian heritage. Her mother had always tried to convince her to widen her perspective and learn more about her full history, but Tabitha refused. She was a wild card with Asian eyes, brown skin, and street in her veins. All of this, and she was still a "pretty girl." Tabitha liked everything cute and yellow, lipstick, foundation, and heels, so it didn't matter what she was doing; Tabitha always dressed up. Janiyah teased her about looking like she was going to the club when she knew they would be sitting in the house.

Everyone had their thing, she guessed. Somehow, hers seemed far worse than everyone else. Tina saw a therapist and took crazy pills, and Miss Bernice let the kids take turns sitting in the passenger's seat of her car. None of that seemed as bad as her situation. Big Sam was dead, but everybody in the hood knows just because the leader dies, doesn't mean you're finished paying your debt. It just passes on to the next person in charge. Her mama may have been strung out and unstable, but she was still her mother, and she still owed. Emotion rose in Janiyah's throat as the women boarded the elevator. She just wanted to get the rest of this money and finish paying her mother's debt, and it would all be over. She had funds, but there was no way she could explain to Tina why she took thousands of dollars out of the account. There was no way Tina could know she worked for Big Sam's people. Janiyah had to earn the money herself. She had to finish the job.

CHAPTER EIGHTEEN

The women boarded the elevator for the fifteenth floor. The old buildings didn't have elevators. There was no need since they were not high-risers, but the renovations added several floors, laundry rooms, and two-bathroom apartments. The structures had fresh green paint, new windows, and more cameras. But none of that mattered in the end. Drug dealers and addicts still ran the projects, and poverty prevailed. Many of the more political residents complained about how the city wasted money on glitter and gold but didn't address the real issues.

Janiyah sighed and Tabitha scratched at her wig.

"Come on now, J, don't start that. We got a new shipment in today, and I don't need you acting all brand new. You know we get paid by the number of bags."

"You know I hate this, Tab."

"I know, baby, but you can be done tonight if you play your cards right. Take that money and never look back."

"I'll do half tonight and come back next week. Make that my last week."

"See, you being lazy."

Janiyah laughed. She couldn't spend that much time here. She had to relieve Miss Bernice soon.

"Dang, we gonna miss you J."

"What about you Tab? Don't you wanna get outta here?"

"And leave all this?" Tabitha twirled around and posed, smiling.

"I'm serious. You ever think about something else?"

"Come on now J. I ain't for the preaching tonight, aiight?"

Janiyah waved her hand. "Aiight."

There was silence between them as the elevator climbed and stopped on the thirteenth floor. A mother and her daughter got on.

"Of course, I think about it," Tab lowered her voice. "But I ain't got a big house in the suburbs and a fancy-ass detective mama to spoil me to death."

"She's not my mother."

"Okay, whatever. You know what I mean. A detective *auntie* who makes sure ya'll don't want for anything.

What do I have? Of course, I *think* about leaving, but for what, J? What's waiting out there for me?"

Janiyah let the silence fill the air. After getting custody over her and her siblings, Tina moved them into that big house in the suburbs while people like Tabitha had to stay here. Tabitha had parents, but after they put her out and abandoned her when they found out she was working for Big Sam, Tabitha didn't want anything to do with them. In return, they don't want anything to do with her either. At least according to Tab. Janiyah had never actually met Tabitha's parents or anyone in her family.

Still, it wasn't fair, and Janiyah hated having to leave her. Janiyah was angry with Tina for taking them away. She thought about her history class, where Professor Grier referred to them as "The Talented Tenth." According to Dubois, the talented tenth was the percentage of blacks who were skilled and intelligent enough to guide the direction of the ninety percent. Grier said they were the leaders of the race. Janiyah shook her head. If every successful black person moved out of the hood, who would be there to help the hood? Janiyah hated to believe that black people abandoned their own when they made it, leaving people like Tabitha feeling like there was no way out. And what did "made it" look like anyway? What did it feel like? They were doing well financially, but here she was on the same elevator, getting ready to do the same thing as Tab.

The elevator opened to floor fifteen, and Janiyah and Tabitha stepped out. *They must live on the sixteenth floor,*

Janiyah thought of the woman and her daughter. The building only had sixteen floors, and everyone knew what the fifteenth floor was all about. The woman gave a side-eye to the young women as they exited.

"What?" Tabitha smacked her lips and rolled her eyes as the elevator doors closed. "Judgmental ass."

The young women walked toward apartment 1502, stopping at apartment 1500, where a large crowd of people stood, some of the workers waiting on the door to 1502 to open, and some of them leechers just there for weed and drinks. They could hear the music booming, the conversation roaring, and the drunken laughter as they got closer. Men and women surrounded the doorway. It was like a party every night at 1500.

"What it looking like in there today?" asked Tabitha as they walked up, speaking to one of the women.

"Same shit."

"I thought we was getting a new shipment in tonight?"

Tabitha wondered why the door to 1502 was still closed. It was time to get down to business. She was all about making extra money. It's how she paid her bills.

"Nah," said a man standing by, "It ain't come yet."

Tabitha laughed when she looked into the man's glossy eyes. "Yo, you on that trip huh?"

"Yeah," said a woman. "He tripping hard. The woman turned her attention to Janiyah. "How you doing lil mama? You good?"

Janiyah forced a smile. "Yeah, I'm straight."

Irritation consumed her as she avoided eye contact with the woman. She couldn't stand being around these people, especially the women. Most everybody had heard stories of her first job and what she used to do. She had to fight off the women just as well as the men.

They stood around and made more idle conversation to pass the time. The apartment door was wide open, and Janiyah and Tabitha walked into a large living room area where people slumped on the couch, already high. Others argued over a game of dominoes at the card table in the middle of the room. Weed smoke and musk filled the air, and drinks were abundant. A woman with short blonde hair approached them, smoking a cigarette.

"They ain't ready yet. Said give them ten minutes to finish the last round. Ya'll eat? Got some wings in the kitchen."

"Hey Mika, girl," said Tabitha hugging her. "We just tryna handle this and be out."

Janiyah and Tabitha had rules. They never ate at 1500 or 1502 and never drank unless it was bottled water. Most of the time, they brought their own drinks. Mama ain't raise no fool.

"I feel you. Niggas got paid today, too, so they high with hard dicks."

Tabitha and Mika laughed, and Janiyah forced a smile. *Damn, can they hurry up?* She turned to look at the door, the group of people still standing around.

"How long they say they gonna be?"

Mika looked Janiyah up and down. "What, you got somewhere you need to be?" The woman stepped back, her eyes roaming Janiyah's body. "Yeah, I heard about you," she smiled, and Tabitha grabbed Mika's arm.

"Chill with that lame-ass shit aiight?"

Mika snatched her arm away and stood back.

"I'm cool. I just think people with histories shouldn't act so uppity is all I'm saying." Mika laughed and walked off.

Janiyah shook her head. "I can't stand that bitch."

The women mingled for a few more minutes until a man they called Big Boi, the head watchman, made the call. Whenever Big Boi yelled, "Aiight!" into the apartment and people scattered, they knew apartment 1502 was open, and it was time.

CHAPTER NINETEEN

Two large men and one woman stopped the girls and searched them before they entered the apartment. They patted their bodies down, checked their hair, their bras, their panties, their shoes, and underneath their tongues. The women were used to the routine, so they instantly got to business. They walked in and removed their shoes, raised their shirts, pulled their pants down and bent over, stuck their tongues out, and shook up their hair. Tabitha had to remove her wig.

It was a spacious apartment, and every room had its walls knocked down to make it even larger. The only rooms they didn't bother were the bathroom and the kitchen. Several long brown tables with brown boxes filled the space. Each box contained four pieces of the product: bagged cocaine, eyedrops, and thirty milliliter plastic bottles of Tropicamide, an antimuscarinic drug that produces dilation of the pupil when applied as eye drops. It is used to allow a better examination of the lens and retina. Boxes of gloves were also present and scattered on the tables. People were already at work and engaged in small talk.

"Look like it's slow today," said Tabitha looking around the room. She would have thought it would be packed with all the people in 1500. Tabitha shrugged *always more leechers than workers*.

Janiyah and Tabitha walked over to their usual spot at the table, always together. Tabitha pulled on her gloves and opened the box in front of her. She pulled out a hand full of baggies, eyedrops, and small bottles of liquid, the Tropicamide, and put a huge pile of it on the table. Next, Tabitha reached for and opened the tiny plastic baggie, the cocaine already in it, and twisted the top of the Tropicamide bottle, opened the eyedrop, and stuck the pointy end into the bottle, sucking up the liquid. Tabitha opened the baggie and squeezed a drop of the fluid in, and snapped the baggie closed. She just made fifty dollars. That's what Tabitha liked about it. It was easy money.

Janiyah repeated Tabitha's actions, along with everyone in the room. It was quiet except for small talk and the moving of boxes, baggies, and bottles opening. The women got lost easily in their work, and Janiyah got lost in thoughts of Ronnie as usual. As she squeezed a drop of the liquid into the baggie, she remembered her first introduction to the drug, the reveal of which Big Sam had warned her to keep her mouth closed. Big

Sam had tied her arms and legs and put duct tape over her mouth. What's worse than being tied up like an animal? Knowing your little brother and sister are in the other room, completely oblivious to what's going on outside of cartoons.

"What's my little mama gonna do now?"

Janiyah remembered seeing her lean against the wall, smoking a blunt. She had ignored Sam's question, her eyes darting around the room. She looked at the driver—that piece of shit. Adam had a big crush on her, and she thought, maybe, she could give him a chance. After finding out about Big Sam, she planned her escape with Mike and Kayla. He was supposed to take them to the bus station. Instead, he brought them right back to Big Sam. Of course, he was working for her. She should have known.

> Come on, Niyah, Sam's voice continued in Janiyah's head, "You had to know I knew you would try and escape me. The good thing though, is that Ronnie ain't that smart."

Janiyah had cringed at the mention of her little brother's name, gritting her teeth against the stickiness of the tape. He was so naïve about Sam.

"He is starting to ask questions, though. I wonder why?"

Big Sam walked up to a man lowering boxes from the top of one of the shelves and into Sam's waiting arms. They were in an undisclosed location, but it looked to Janiyah to be a warehouse with rooms. A table sat in the center, and large boxes sat on shelves. She was sure it was where they did their dirty work. The man handed Sam a large container, and she sat it on the table.

"I'm sure you'll keep your mouth shut about what you see here."

A knock at the door startled Janiyah out of her thoughts and made everyone's heads turn toward the sound. People didn't knock on that door. If workers arrived, they were escorted into the apartment by Big Boi and then searched just as Janiyah and Tabitha had been. If they weren't welcomed, they wouldn't be let in. There was never a knock at the door except for one occasion, and everyone knew what that occasion was. The boss lady was here, the woman who replaced Big Sam.

A tall, heavy-set Puerto Rican woman entered the room. Her hair was styled as it always was, French braided up and pulled into a ponytail. She wore a white t-shirt, baggy blue jeans, and fresh Air Jordans. Tattoos covered both her arms and an eyebrow ring dotted her left brow. The room looked up in familiarity, some of the people spoke as she entered. Everyone knew Renita. Known around the way as Rita, Renita and Big Sam were besties and it was common knowledge she would most likely take over Sam's operation. She had been low-key, sucking up all she could from her mentor. Rarely were they not seen together and most importantly, Rita had no record and was not on the FBI's radar.

She walked in and placed her fists on the table, leaning in, commanding everyone's attention without speaking. She got straight to the point. Her motive was never to beat around the bush.

"Okay, good people. Ya'll be putting in good work, but I'm here because I need you to go harder. I put an order in for a stronger dose of Tropicamide, and you will do two drops instead of one."

Whispers of disagreement floated around the room and gave birth to the tension Janiyah felt in her bones.

"This bitch crazy," a young woman whispered, speaking what was on everyone's mind.

Renita looked in the woman's direction, and the room quieted. She smiled. "The boxes are on the way. Start adding the new doses tomorrow."

"No, disrespect Rita," spoke a man in the back. "But niggas are out here going crazy for this stuff already. I mean, the cocaine already strong, but this Tropicamide?"

"I agree," said the woman who whispered, "People are out of their minds with it. It's doing something to their eyes. We are finding corpses in the building every day all sucked in and creepy-looking and shit."

"Ya'll heard about that Steakhouse case, right?" asked the man.

Everyone nodded. It was apparent the men were high off trip. That's what they called the drug. Popular catchphrases like "You tripping" took on a whole new meaning, and mixing the Tropicamide with cocaine produced an extremely potent high. Every day there were news reports of people dying all over the city. They found corpses everywhere, in stairwells, dark alleys, apartments, and women holding crying babies as they nodded off. The most famous case was the Steakhouse incident, where three men were found dead at the El Che Steakhouse and Bar. The Feds were hollering murder, but the streets called it trip. People were starting to do it in broad daylight, half of them not even bothering to mix it right. It was 1982 all over again, and trip was the new crack.

Renita was silent a long time, and everyone looked around in confusion. And then, she smiled. Again.

This doesn't look good, Janiyah thought. Nothing about Renita's smile was good.

Renita put her hands in her pockets and stared at the man and woman.

"The corpses are an eyesore. We'll handle that."

Janiyah looked at Tabitha, who shrugged her shoulders. Rita didn't agree with anything. Something was definitely up.

"You two. Follow me," she said to the young man and woman. "The rest of you, back to work."

The man and the woman shrugged and followed Renita out of the apartment.

"Dumbasses," murmured Tabitha as she filled another bag.

Janiyah kept working, but Tab was right. Jojo and Lexi speaking out was a stupid move. If you left the room with Rita, you never came back. Smart people knew where they went, but there was no funeral. There were never any funerals. Not unless you were some big shot, celebrity, or politician. But if you came from Altgeld and the murder was suspected of being drug-related, the most you got was a missing person poster on the refrigerator in your mother's kitchen. *Rita agreed with them, though. Maybe they'll be back.*

Janiyah picked up another baggie and watched the door. *Maybe.*

Big Sam signaled the man standing next to a closed room door, he knocked. “Aye,” he shouted, letting the person on the other side know it was time.

Janiyah rocked the chair so furiously that it tipped over, and she crashed onto the floor, her face hitting the concrete first, her nose and mouth bleeding underneath the tape and sliding down her chin. Janiyah screamed from the pain in her jaw and from the pain of what she was seeing. It was her baby sister Kayla, blindfolded with a gun to her head.

The man walked the little girl closer to Janiyah, and tears spilled from her eyes. Big Sam smirked.

“As I said, I’m sure you’ll keep your mouth shut about what you see.”

Big Sam walked over to Janiyah and ripped the tape from her mouth, and specks of blood flew off with it. Sam cringed and wiped the droplets that landed on her hand off on her jeans."

"Please!" cried Janiyah, "Please don't hurt her!"

"It was just a matter of time before you told Ronnie about our little investment."

At the mention of Ronnie's name, a sound is heard near the door.

That's not really what happened next, but it always ended this way, missing all the other stuff that happened in-between. The same scene played itself on a loop in her mind. Ronnie emerges from behind the door, points a gun at Big Sam, she smiles, and Janiyah screams.

"Ronnie, no!"

Janiyah jumped up into a sitting position, the blaring sound of the alarm ringing. She reached over and slammed her hand against the clock to silence it and tugged against the t-shirt she wore to bed, tears brimming her eyes. She looked at the clock. It was four in the morning. She shook her head. It was the same nightmare and the same scene. Why couldn't she remember anything else? It always skipped to the part when Ronnie pulled the trigger, but she never sees him fall. Should she be thankful? Hell no. Janiyah was upset with God, the Universe, or whoever it was controlling things up there. Not seeing her brother die but replaying the moment just before he did was no favor. Tina would always come to her rescue, rocking her back and forth. *She thinks I'm a saint*. Janiyah was thankful her mother's bestie had taken them in, but there was so much she didn't know. Janiyah blamed herself for Ronnie's death. If it weren't for her sneaking around with Tabitha to work for Big Sam, he would have never been involved.

What happened that night was a tragedy. Two people lost their lives, and one of them was her baby brother. But what did she miss? There had to be something about the dreams other than the trauma she experienced from witnessing her brother's death.

***

Big Boi, who held onto Jojo, and another guy around the way named Moose, who held onto Lexi, and Renita walked the hallway to an apartment on the first floor, where another tall, husky man greeted them. He saw Renita, nodded, and opened the door to the apartment. Plush cardinal red carpet greeted the five as they entered.

"Take those shoes off. Ya'll know better."

The tall and slender man puffed on a cigar. He wore a two-piece suit as usual, and his hair cascaded down his back, always in a ponytail and braided like a thick, black rope. His smooth, reddish skin didn't have a scratch on it except for one long keloid scar that made a trail from his right eye down the right side of his face and stopped underneath his chin. For this reason, everyone called him Scar.

Scar smiled and let the cigar hang from his lips as he and Renita greeted with a handshake.

"'Sup, shorty."

A large red oak desk sat in the center of the apartment. Like 1502, this apartment was cleared out and used as one ample office space, though the rooms were kept intact. On top of the desk sat a stack of books, binders, and other supplies. Two matching red oak chairs sat in front of the desk. On the walls were photographs of children, men, women, and people in the community, and behind the desk, sat a large self-portrait of Scar, the muscle behind Big Sam's operation. He was a hidden hand, the head of Renita. No one who was not high ranking in the organization even knew his real name.

Scar sat in the chair behind the desk and stretched out his long legs as Renita, Big Boi, and Moose stood back, pushing Jojo and Lexi closer to Scar's desk. Lexi cried.

Scar put his cigar out in the gold-plated ashtray in front of him and nodded toward the door.

"I got it from here."

Renita, Big Boi, and Moose left the room, and Jojo hung his head low. Lexi's cries got louder.

"Please," she begged.

"Don't beg. It is unbecoming," he smiled, "Have a seat."

Jojo and Lexi eyed each other and then looked at Scar.

"I don't repeat myself."

Quickly, the two sat in the chairs facing the desk.

"What seems to be the problem?"

"Nothing, man. We was tripping, man. I mean. We wasn't *tripping*. Like, we not on trip. We were tripping like bugging out. Know what I'm saying…?"

Scar raised a hand and Jojo stopped rambling.

"Please, Mr. Scar. We didn't mean to be disrespectful," cried Lexi.

Scar lit his cigar again, puffed on it and blew out smoke.

"You are going to make this up to me."

"You're not gonna kill us?"

"Lexi, man. Chill out," whispered Jojo.

Scar shook his head. "Listen. I got this pet cat."

Jojo and Lexi looked at each other again.

"Cat...?" asked Jojo.

Scar put out his cigar, sat back in the chair, and retrieved a small Crown Royal bottle from the bottom drawer of his desk and a plastic cup.

"Ya'll drink?"

Jojo and Lexi quickly shook their heads.

Scar poured the drink into the cup and the crisp smell of the alcohol floated into the air.

He inhaled, "That's too bad," he said, quickly taking a shot. He refilled the cup and then put the bottle back into the drawer. Scar stood and walked over to the window. One hand held onto the cup, and the other hand he placed in his pants pocket. The man was relentless and had zero tolerance for bullshit. He didn't hesitate to make an example out of people who got in his way. He stayed three steps ahead at all times. He nicknamed Big Sam, and he decided to put her out front. He knew the name would confuse the cops who would mistake her for being a man. If they were looking for a man named Sam, they weren't looking at Samantha, and if they weren't looking at Samantha, they weren't looking at him. And if they weren't looking at him, they weren't looking at *her*. The thought of *her* made him smile, and the hairs stand up on his neck. He swallowed the remains of his drink. She was his only weakness.

"Yes," he said facing them. "A big-ass cat. I keep it locked up, but it is getting hungry."

Jojo and Lexi frowned.

"All I want you to do for me is feed it."

Terror flashed across Lexi's face as she looked into Jojo's eyes.

"What...what do cats eat...eat," stammered Jojo.

Scar called for his officers and Big Boi and Moose walked in. Moose stood behind Lexi, and Big Boi stood behind Jojo. The kids looked frantically around, and Scar emptied the contents of his drink.

"Meat."

"Scar please just hear us out…"

Jojo pleaded but was too late for Big Boi's arms. Moose followed the lead, grabbing an already-crying Lexi.

"No, please! We sorry! We sorry, Scar!" she screamed. Moose lifted her from the chair in one scoop, walking her to the back room screaming and kicking.

Jojo kicked and tried punching Big Boi, but his efforts were no match for Big Boi's arms. He put the boy in a headlock, dragged him to the back, and threw him into an empty bedroom. Moose followed through and threw Lexi into the same room, and slammed the door closed. Moose and Big Boi nodded at Scar as they walked out of the apartment.

Scar heard the screams coming from the back room, and he winced at the sounds. As much as he had done this before, he could never get used to the sound of *her* feeding.

He stood next to the window as he always had and waited until the temperature in the room rose and the hairs on his arms stood up.

"You handle yourself well."

"Friday night after the move. Make it look like some innocent bystander thing. You know how to do it."

CHAPTER TWENTY-ONE

Eddie wiped the sweat from his forehead, swiped the rope from side to side, and then jumped it. He had been doing this the past ten minutes. Jason punched the bag, stopping to catch it as it swung back to him.

"I don't know, man. Funerals are expensive as hell. I wanted to do a combined thing, but I think we can do something for Steve and call it a day. The rest of them got families. Know what I'm saying?"

Jason pushed the emotion back down his throat. Big Steve was his brother and, unlike the others, had no one. He struck at the bag in a series of punches. Eddie stopped jumping and grabbed a water bottle.

"Man, I know. How much you think we can get from the fundraiser?"

Jason was quiet a moment, punched the bag some more, and walked off.

"As much as we can. It's gonna be at least ten stacks to bury him. Speaking of which, I gotta meet with some dude. Already running late. You still looking into that DJ guy, right?"

"Yeah. Homeboy, my cousin on my daddy's side. Said he can hook us up with a lil something and host it at the park over there by 47th."

Jason punched the bag again, "The A?"

"What nigga? It's free!"

"Naw man. Find somebody else."

"Come on, man."

"Eddie, we not hosting a fundraiser at the projects."

"First, it's not the projects. It's the park next to the projects. And secondly, what? You too good for the hood?"

Jason laughed. "No, man. But they are already trying to say fam was on drugs. Linking up with those wanna-be gangsta niggas in the A is not a good look."

"Everybody in the A ain't no wanna-be gangsta bro."

Jason dropped his shoulders. He had touched a nerve. Eddie moved out of Altgeld years ago, but his half-brother still lived there.

"Sorry, bro. I know that's a soft spot for you, but you gotta dig where I'm coming from, too."

"How about this…won't you just meet him?"

"I'll think about it," said Jason laughing as he walked off. "But meeting him ain't changing my mind!"

***

Jason's leg bounced up and down at the bar. He sipped his beer and looked at his watch for the third time. He was meeting with a financial planner to help with the fundraiser.

"Man, where is this cat?"

Just as he was about to curse the man out in his head, an Hispanic man wearing a black suit and holding onto a briefcase approached him. The man extended his hand. Jason looked him up and down.

"Jason."

"Alex."

Jason raised a brow. "How tall are you, man?"

"Pretty tall."

Jason laughed. "I know you played ball."

"No."

Jason expected the man to say more, but he didn't. He brushed off the awkwardness with a laugh.

"Man get outta here."

"I hear you are looking to raise some money."

"Most definitely."

"What would you say is the estimate?"

"Imma need at least ten stacks."

"Ten thousand dollars is a lot of money to raise."

Jason picked his glass up and drank his beer. "So are funerals."

"I think I can help you, but I have to be honest. My name is not Alex."

Jason put the glass down. "Look man. I ain't got time for no nonsense."

"I'm actually here with someone."

The man removed a cell phone from his pocket and put it to his ear. As it rang, he hoped Jason wouldn't punch him in the face. The scowl he was making said that he would.

"You can come in now."

Jason tilted his head as the person walked into the bar.

"What the hell is this?"

Tina walked up to the bar wearing a pair of blue jeans, black t-shirt, baseball cap, sneakers, and sunglasses.

"I can explain."

"Then do it," said Jason through clenched teeth.

Tina lowered her voice. "Not here."

Jason shook his head, cut his eyes at the tall man who said his name wasn't Alex, and got up from the bar.

The three walked out of the bar and to Tina's car where she removed the glasses.

"Jason, Az. Az, Jason," she said pointing.

Jason's face turned red, and his frown deepened. "I'm trying to plan a fucking funeral Tina!"

"I know that's why I wanted you to meet him."

Jason shook his head. The woman had gone insane. "I see you still on that bullshit. You said Az was an angel, alien, or some shit. Not a tall-ass man who said he never played basketball even though there's no way in hell he…"

"Jason…"

"… didn't because you can't be that tall and not at least show the slightest interest in basketball…"

"Jason!" Tina screamed, shaking him.

"Don't touch me."

"Look behind you."

Jason shook his head and turned around. "Oh, shit," he said, stumbling back, raising his fists into the air.

Tina went to stand next to Az, now twelve feet tall. His eyes were bulbs of blue light.

"This," said Tina, "Is Azbuga, the Watcher Archangel I've been telling you about," she said, smiling.

"This shit ain't funny."

"I am sorry about your friends."

Jason looked the angel up and down. "Yeah aiight. How I know you ain't kill them?"

"So, you do believe that fallen angels killed them."

Jason turned away from Az and faced Tina. "I ain't say all that."

Jason thought about the weird feeling he picked up from that woman that night at the apartment and his father's warning about hoodoo magic. He brushed it off. *This woman gonna have me going crazy.*

"They killed Ronnie, too."

Jason turned back around to face Az and jumped again. He had shrunk back down to six feet.

"Man, stop doing that."

"Sorry."

"I don't need you to apologize. Just stop doing it."

Tina shook her head, "I keep telling him that."

"Look, I'm supposed to be meeting this man about a fundraiser, so I'd appreciate it if we can hurry this up."

"Jason, there is no man. Az is your guy."

"We can manipulate technology, shapeshift, and…"

"…let me guess, read minds?"

"Yes. We read energy. We can tell where you will be and read your thoughts based on the energy you are giving off. That's how Paschar knows where to find you before your next move."

"Who the hell is Paschar?"

"Angel of vision," said Tina.

Jason shook his head. "This some wild shit."

"Paschar is a powerful fallen angel," said Az. "You must not underestimate her. She is a witch who uses sex energy to extract energy from a mortal and uses her eyes to project illusions."

"What does all this have to do with me?"

"Her legion is responsible for the deaths of your friends."

"And the death of Ronnie," Tina added.

"She almost killed you once. She will try to do it again."

"Wait, what? When?"

"That night at the apartment."

Jason put his hand over his mouth. "*That's* Paschar?"

Tina shook her head, "Yup."

"Damn." *That girl was fine, thick, and sexy.*

"I was able to get to her before she sucked you dry but she hasn't stopped following you."

"Sucked me dry?" Jason laughed.

Tina touched Jason's arm. "Don't think of it sexually."

Jason's anger raged within him. He was still upset with her for getting him into this.

"So, what we do now?"

"Apparently, there's a door still open at Altgeld," said Tina.

"The PJs?"

Jason thought about Eddie's invitation to meet his homeboy there.

"There is something connecting you both to Altgeld," said Az, "Which is leaving a door open."

Jason folded his arms. "You the big bad angel. Won't you just tell us what the door is so we can close it?"

"He can't."

"Why not?"

Tina shrugged. "It's against the rules or something."

"Rules?"

Jason rubbed his temples. “My head hurts.”

“Me and Az got a plan, and we were hoping you could help.”

“You say this thing is trying to kill me. What choice do I have? I just want whatever the hell this is to be over so I can bury my friend and get back to my little girl.”

“The first thing you need to do is call your friend. Tell him you’ll meet with Moose.”

Jason looked up at Az. He still couldn’t believe he was an alien, angel, or whatever.

“Who the hell is Moose?”

“The friend of your friend.”

CHAPTER TWENTY-TWO

Hitomi floated into the warehouse through the window and lowered herself to the floor. Her black leather bodysuit fit the Korean body well, hiding her actual mermaid image, and her eyes cast a blue light on everything it touched. She shivered in the skin and frowned at the smell of hot metal and decay. The warehouse was vacant, and the floors shined like new, but the spirit of Big Sam slept in the walls. Hitomi licked her lips at the taste of ancient blood. Tyrone White. Everyone knew his name. He was a popular subject among principalities. His sacrifice killed Big Sam, sending her spirit to Tartarus, the prison for spirits beneath the Earth.

Hitomi passed by blurred windows smudged with dirt and dust and moldy walls with water stains. Slivers of light shone from the outside and fought with the blue rays of her eyes. Hitomi winced and covered her face.

"That is why I said to wear shades."

Hitomi inched closer to the center of the room where Paschar stood wearing sunglasses and a red pantsuit. Her chocolate skin was beautiful. Hitomi was jealous. Everyone was. Pas always got the best skin.

"It is time to move on. Altgeld has served its purpose. We've been infiltrated."

Hitomi raised a brow. "What?"

"They are not all human."

"Do we know who the perpetrator is?"

"No, but I am sure Az has something to do with it. He's a pain in my ass."

"What about the Janiyah girl?"

"No. She is flesh."

Hitomi cleared her throat. "No, I mean. What do we do with her? She's our connection to Big Sam's spirit."

Paschar frowned. "We've been over this."

"I know but…"

"You're not developing human feelings on me, are you?"

Hitomi swallowed hard. She was the descendant of Atargatis, goddess of the moon, feminine power, and water, who became a mermaid after inadvertently causing her mortal lover's death and then trying to drown herself. Instead of drowning, she turned into a mermaid, a woman with the tail of a fish. Like the mermaids before her, Hitomi was worshipped in a temple made of gold with a pool. Worshippers would swim through the pool to get to her altar. She filled the pool with living fish, an animal they deemed sacred, representing fertility and bounty. For centuries Hitomi fed on the souls of those who swam in her pool until she met *him*. She fell in love with a mortal man who had come to worship in her pool and, like the goddess before her, accidentally caused his death. Mortal men were her weakness, and Paschar was not going to let her live it down.

Hitomi straightened her back. "No. Of course not."

Paschar looked into the eyes of her contemporary with a tight-lipped smile and unconvincing eyes. She turned away from Hitomi and faced one of the dust-covered windows, the light in her eye protected by the shades against the natural light of the sun.

"Do you remember the story?"

Hitomi dropped her shoulders, faced the ceiling, shook her head, and folded her arms. "Of course."

"Our fathers, children of heaven, two hundred of them, our leaders, assembled on Mount Hermon. They swore an oath and bound themselves by it. They were loyal, dedicated."

Paschar paused and turned to face Hitomi.

"Faithful."

She said the word without leaving Hitomi's eyes and turned back toward the window.

"They had one mind and one goal. To make life better for humans. How much more powerful did they become when our ancestors mixed their powerful angelic spirits with their blood?"

Hitomi shifted. She knew this story too well. They all did. Paschar's recounting of it was unnecessary but she knew better not to stop her. Pas was bitter. They all knew that.

Paschar turned away from the window to face Hitomi.

"Azazel taught them to make swords, and knives, and shields, breastplates, and made known to them the metals of the Earth and the art of working them. Bracelets and ornaments and the beautifying of the eyelids. Semjaza too, who taught enchantments and root-cuttings, and Armaros the resolving of those enchantments. Baraqijal taught them astrology and Ezeqeel the knowledge of the clouds. Our leaders imparted new and profound knowledge to the humans of the Earth, and how does *he* repay us?"

Paschar was breathing hard, glimpses of her real image fading in and out. She noticed the annoying facial expression Hitomi wore and calmed.

"We were created first, and yet he refers to them as being *made in his image*. Can you believe it? Rotting flesh made in the image of spirit. It's pathetic."

Hitomi looked down at the floor reflectively. She had heard stories of how the angels perished, with their cries reaching up to the heavens. She pushed the human emotion aside and resurrected the anger still present at the pit of her stomach. Paschar was right. Something needed to be done. These angels taught humanity everything they knew, even doing away with the baby in the womb. An abortion the humans called it, from the Latin word abortionem.

Having divided themselves into chiefs of ten, Hitomi and her girls were among the many descendants of these ancient aliens. They even had mixed children among the human population, demi-gods created of both spirit and blood, and still, it was not enough. The Almighty disapproved of their marrying human men and women and inventing new things. Nothing was ever enough for *him*.

"These were our ancestors," continued Paschar. "And we owe it to their legacy to avenge their demise. No one lives."

CHAPTER TWENTY-THREE

Janiyah looked down at her phone.

"Shit, girl! I gotta go."

Tabitha and Janiyah were standing on the patio, five doors down from 1502. They had finished bagging and spent the rest of the time hanging out. It was going on 10:30 pm and Janiyah had to relieve Miss Bernice. Tina had texted her earlier to say she wouldn't make it in time. Janiyah promised she'd be there. She needed to leave now.

"Why don't you just chill here?"

Janiyah frowned. "You must have gotten a contact if you think Imma spend a night here."

"You must have gotten a contact if you think I meant 1502!"

They laughed.

"You can crash at my crib or at Tanya's. You know how we do."

"I don't know girl. I like my bed. Besides, I need to get there and relieve Miss Bernice."

"This late?"

"Girl, Tina been tripping, and I don't mean *tripping*. She been bugging out for real. Coming in all late. I been relieving Miss Bernice on the low."

"Maybe she got a man. Good dick will do it to you. Have you coming in late, cooking, cleaning, looking all cross-eyed and shit. Just toxic."

Janiyah laughed out loud. "Girl you crazy."

"Don't I know it," laughed Tabitha.

"But for real…she got a man?"

Janiyah frowned. "Girl I don't know. Probably."

Tabitha lifted her head and saw someone approaching from the stairwell.

"Hey, Kenneth!" she waved.

The boy pushed his backpack over his shoulder and nodded.

"'Sup, Tab. Hey, Niyah."

Janiyah waved. "Hey, Kenneth." She smiled but said nothing more. Kenneth had a crush on her, but she wasn't interested. He had a friendly face and cute dimples, an attractive smile, and dressed okay for a non-gang member. He had a part-time job at Walgreens around the corner and was smart. He was just the kind of boy Tina would want her to date, and it was why he wasn't her type.

Tabitha frowned. "What you doing up here?"

"Elevator broke again."

Tabitha shook her head. "Should have known. Come on. We going down. You can roll with us."

Kenneth walked to the middle of the hall, and the three took the nearest stairwell. The new Altgeld high-risers consisted of apartments on one side of the patio and gates on the other side. There were two stairwells, one on each end of the floor, an incinerator, and on the side of the gates in the middle were the elevators.

Janiyah cut her eyes at Tabitha, who smiled as the three of them walked down the steps.

"How long you here?" asked Kenneth.

Janiyah laughed. "For about five more minutes. You know I can't kick it here."

"True. I don't blame you. Hey, my mom's making chicken. You know how she does it. You are both welcomed to stop in."

"I think I just said I couldn't kick it here," joked Janiyah, but her stomach growled anyway. Miss Vicky made the best fried chicken in the building. *But I gotta relieve Miss Bernice.*

"Now you *know* we want some chicken!"

Kenneth laughed at Tabitha as they made it to the eighth floor.

"Okay."

Janiyah waved them off. "Ya'll go ahead. I gotta hit it."

"At least take a plate home. Besides, you know I can't let you walk down there by yourself."

Kenneth was in love with Janiyah, but he wasn't going to tell her. He liked her, but he knew girls like her. He had seen her around some of the biggest names in the streets. He knew they protected her, and his mother had warned him about girls like her. *Got all these hood niggas protecting her? Yeah, you leave that alone.*

Despite his mother's warnings, he couldn't help his feelings, even if she was probably only into the bad boy type. He liked her mainly because she was different. Like him, she didn't belong here. He could tell. Like everyone, he had heard stories of her past, how she used to strip for women who worked for Big Sam, but he didn't judge her for it, unlike everyone else.

"Yeah, J. You *know* he can't let you do that."

Janiyah frowned at Tabitha, who laughed as they approached apartment 809. The delicious smell of grease and seasoning wafted through the air and entered their nostrils. Kenneth took out his keys and unlocked the door.

"Moms will make you a plate, and I'll walk you down. Plus, you know she made the garlic mashed potatoes, too, with the sweet corn."

Janiyah sighed. *Not the sweet corn.*

***

"Thank you for walking us down, I appreciate it, but you don't have to do this."

"Yeah, you don't have to do this," said Tabitha, nudging her friend.

Kenneth shook his head.

"I said I was walking you down and I'm a man of my word."

Tabitha smacked her lips, "I don't know about the man part but aiight."

Janiyah laughed. "Thank you, Kenny. I appreciate it."

"You're welcome, beautiful," Kenneth winked and then turned to leave. "Catch up with ya'll later."

"Later," the women said in unison, walking over to Janiyah's Jeep. She got in and rolled down the window.

"I thought you was helping Miss Vicky?"

Tabitha waved. "Girl, I can't."

The women laughed. Miss Vicky never stopped talking. Her dad, Kenneth's grandfather, was a member of the Black Panthers, Chicago division, and she made sure everyone knew it. Miss Vicky talked about black unity back then, the panther's origin, how they met Fred Hampton and Huey Percy Newton that one time—always calling him by his whole name so people would know she knew him. She talked about how the Panthers got started every chance she got, their food program, their healthcare program with the sickle cell anemia testing, their ten-point program, and community activism. They didn't know how Kenneth survived in that house.

"No. What is up with Kenny though?"

Tabitha leaned against the window of the car as Janiyah put the key into the ignition. She shrugged.

"Same ole Kenny I guess."

"Something's up with him."

Janiyah frowned. "What you mean?"

"What was he doing on the fifteenth floor?"

"Girl, you know them elevators always broke."

"The more I teach you, the dumber you get."

"What? I already know he like me."

"Bitch, how the elevator stops on the fifteenth floor, and you live on the eighth? Did he push the wrong button?

"I didn't even think about it like that."

"The elevators stay broke, but you know they never make it this far up when they get stuck. Usually, you have to walk up but not down."

Janiyah shook her head. "Right."

"If Kenny was taking the elevator up, what business does he have on the fifteenth floor?"

Janiyah's eyebrows raised. "You think he dealing trip?"

Tabitha stood back from the truck and looked around, "I don't know," her eyes met Janiyah's. "But he dealing something."

Janiyah shook her head. "Nah. Kenny not the type."

"Which is exactly why he prime for recruit because he *ain't the type.*"

CHAPTER TWENTY-FOUR

Scar returned to taking care of some paperwork at his desk, but his mind was still on Hitomi's orders. Something wasn't right. Tomorrow was Friday. He picked up the phone.

"Rita. Yeah. Meeting at eight o'clock. Sharp. Yes, in the morning. Tell everybody."

Scar hung up the phone and returned to his work when the temperature in the room increased. He was not afraid of anyone. No one made him nervous, not even Hitomi, but the room felt different. The presence felt like Hitomi's, but the energy was different. Darker.

He felt an energy floating around him and fought the mixture of fear and arousal that had come over him thick like a blanket. He stood up quickly, away from his desk and to the middle of the room, snatching himself from the aura.

"Who are you?"

Paschar appeared, her skin looked wet, and the red jumpsuit hugged every crevice of her body in all the right places.

"Hello, Scar."

"Who are you, and what are you doing in my apartment?"

Paschar laughed. "This hasn't been your apartment in years."

She fake pouted and leaned in close, her booty rubbing up against his crouch.

"Do you trust her?"

"What?"

The entity walked around the apartment, touching the photographs on the wall and enjoying the surge of energy she felt from the people in the pictures, watching glimpses of their lives from the internal screen of her eyes. She stepped back.

"Oh, don't play innocent with me, Mister. I know you've been seeing her."

Scar loosened his tie, wiping the sweat from his face.

"Oh? She didn't tell you about me? Well now, that's a pity."

"What do you want?"

Paschar walked up to Scar and cupped his manhood, hard against his jeans.

"I've seen you in action. Impressive."

She gripped harder, and the pleasure turned to pain. Scar pushed against the woman, but she was like solid rock.

"Man, what the fuck…?"

"She's getting weak, ya know."

Scar writhed in pain.

"Her energy is off, Scar."

She let him go, and Scar stumbled. "Shit," he cursed under his breath, holding his genitalia.

Paschar floated around the room.

"You are not her first, you know."

Scar charged at the entity full speed after a moment of recovery, but Paschar's eyes turned into black holes, and her teeth grew long and sharp. Her body rose to the height of the ceiling, and her voice deepened. She held out her arm, and it stretched from across the room, catching Scar by the throat, his body suspended in the air. Scar's body twisted and turned, his arms trying to release Paschar's grip from his neck. He should have known it was too good to be true when Hitomi walked up to him that day. He had never had a woman so down about the drug game. He thought she was legit interested in being his right hand and those eyes. Those eyes were unlike anything he'd ever seen. He felt sure he had her, and when he saw her pure form, oddly enough, it turned him on even more. Never in a million years would he have thought demons, devils, and angels were ruling Sam's enterprise. Scar cursed himself for allowing Hitomi to get under his skin and mix the Tropicamide with the cocaine. Trip wasn't just a drug; it was sorcery. It was how Paschar and her legion sucked the souls of people right out of their bodies when they weren't doing it manually. Drug enterprises weren't just about getting high; they were witchcraft. Scar regretted finding out too late about this spiritual warfare.

The entity vanished, and Scar fell on his face, hitting his head against the carpeted floor that now, oddly, felt like concrete. A pool of blood hemorrhaged from his head.

CHAPTER TWENTY-FIVE

Tina slammed the door behind her, but it didn't close all the way, so Amy and other co-workers assembled at the door, anxious for a whiff of office gossip. Juan hung up the phone, his eyes wide as Tina slammed the phone face-up on his desk.

"Another one."

"What are you doing here?"

"Look at it."

Juan shook his head. He looked at the door where a small crowd had gathered.

"Close that door."

Tina turned to close the door but not without a staredown with Amy, who rolled her eyes and walked away.

She returned to Juan's desk and sat down in one of the chairs. Juan picked up the phone, staring at the headlines, his blood pressure rising as he read on:

Sean "Scar" Carver, 33,

Dead at Altgeld

Juan put the phone down and rubbed at his eyes with his thumb.

"What is this Tina?"

"I don't know. You tell me what it is."

"I don't have time for this."

Tina got up and paced the floor.

"People are out here losing their lives! We have yet to solve the Byron case and there are already dozens more on top of that."

"T, go home. You are still suspended, which means that I cannot legally discuss any open case with you."

Tina shook her head, "You are unbelievable."

Juan shrugged. "Don't take it personal."

Jason read the headlines on his phone and set it down on the coffee table in front of him. It was late, and somehow Tina was in his apartment. He dreamed about this day, only not like this.

"You gotta stop this."

Tina frowned. "You too?"

"No, I mean this detective shit. You gotta stop going to Juan."

"What do you mean?"

Jason stood. "You know, you the dumbest smart person I've ever met."

Tina folded her arms.

"This ain't no damn case. Not anymore."

Tina rolled her eyes.

"You mean to tell me you been hanging around some blue-eyed alien…"

"Angel."

"Angel, whatever. You have been hanging around this dude this whole time, and you still ain't figured it out yet."

Tina crossed her legs.

"Paschar keeps killing brothers, and the cops ain't doing a damn thing about it. This is some next level shit T. We in some kinda supernatural war, and right now Paschar or whatever the hell her name is…she's winning."

Tina covered her face with her hands. It was true. Paschar's kills did not show any sign of slowing down, and the Feds still couldn't figure the Byron thing out. Sure, she knew it was a legion of fallen angel women, but that's not something you can produce as evidence to the cops. Frustration gripped her, and Tina couldn't help the tears from falling.

Jason sat back on the sofa and held her in his arms.

"Let it out Ma. You been holding that shit in too long."

As Tina sobbed in his arms, Jason caressed her hair and rubbed her back. Tina looked up into his eyes and brushed her lips across his. Jason kissed her deeply but pulled back. He held her at length. Tina's eyes searched his.

"I'm. I'm sorry," she stammered. "I didn't mean to…"

"No," said Jason. "It's not that. Look, you gotta go."

Tina's eyebrows shot up, and she stood. Her heart sank, and she was gripped by self-consciousness. *Was she that bad of a kisser? Was she too forward?* She hadn't been this interested in a guy since Malachi, the first person to teach her about *them*. Tina grabbed her things and headed for the door. If she hurried, she could make it out to the car without crying.

Jason caught her at the door.

"Look, I like you, but my daughter ain't met you yet. As I said, it's nothing personal. This is just not the right time. We gotta stay focused, and I can't focus while you here," he winked.

Tina fake smiled, waved, and hurried out of the door. The loyalty this man was showing toward his daughter and the respect he had for them both was turning her on even more.

CHAPTER TWENTY-SIX

Janiyah pulled up to the house and parked in her usual spot. "Dammit," she said, looking up at the beautiful brick house. It wasn't so beautiful now, though. The kitchen light was still on, which meant either Miss Bernice was still there, or Tina was home. Janiyah picked up the pace, inserted the key into the door, and rushed in. She didn't even see Tina standing on the top of the stairs until she hung up her jacket.

"Where you been?" Tina asked, sitting on a stair.

"I'm sorry for being late T. It won't happen again."

"I'm glad. But that's not my question." Tina held up a hand. "And before you lie to me, it's been a long day, and I am not in the mood. I'm so tired I'm not even mad. I just wanna know where you been."

Janiyah took out her phone and started scrolling. “I was at Tabitha’s.”

“Janiyah, put the phone down. We are having a conversation.”

Janiyah sighed, sat the phone on the kitchen counter, and folded her arms.

“We had an agreement about this, didn’t we?”

“Yeah, but…”

“…I told you I’m not in the mood for excuses or lies tonight. I also remember telling you I don’t want you hanging around that godforsaken place.”

Janiyah rolled her eyes, but Tina ignored it.

“What reason do you have to hang out there? What’s been with you lately? We used to talk all the time. What’s up? What’s going on?”

“Nothing,” Janiyah scratched at her head. *This conversation is tired.*

“So why you got this attitude like *I* missed *my* curfew?”

“I’m not a baby T. You don’t have to talk to me like that.”

“Apparently, I do.”

Janiyah sucked her teeth. *Sick of this shit.* “You know what T? *You* are what’s wrong.”

Tina raised a brow. “Is that right?”

"You are coming at me like I'm some kinda kid, but you the one coming in all late, never have time for nobody no more. I have been relieving Miss Bernice on my own. *I* have been putting the kids to bed, and *I* have been spending time with them while you are out doing who knows what…"

"That's enough," said Tina raising a hand. "You said your piece."

Janiyah could see the fire in Tina's eyes and the bruised ego too. *Good. Now she knows how we feel.*

"Look, I'm sorry. I have been MIA a lot lately. That's on me. I'm sorry you feel neglected. You know that's not my intention."

"Is it a man? You dating or something? What?" Janiyah walked over to the stairs and sat. She really wanted to know what had her aunt's attention after she vowed to be there for them.

Tina smiled.

"I knew it!" laughed Janiyah. "What's his name?"

"No, no. It's nothing like that. We are working a case together."

Janiyah waved. "His name young lady."

"His name is Jason," laughed Tina.

"Ooh. I like it. *Jason*. Got a sexy ring to it."

"Cut it out," waved Tina.

Janiyah smiled but not because Tina finally had a man. Tabitha had told her that much. She smiled because she had diverted attention away from Tabitha. Tina's next round of questioning could have been brutal. She couldn't find out about her working for Big Sam's people. Especially not before tomorrow. It was their big day with the new shipment, and she needed to put in as much time as necessary to have enough money to quit finally. She was almost finished paying off her mama's debt, and she wasn't going to let anything stop her mission.

"I'm going to bed, but I need you home earlier. Miss Bernice was pissed."

"Did she quit?"

Tina cut her eyes, standing. "Damn near."

"Miss Bernice ain't gonna quit. The money too good."

Tina walked down the stairs. "I guess." She walked through the kitchen and was no longer visible.

"Hey, what time you need me here tomorrow?"

"I don't know yet," yelled Tina from the back. "Just be here early!"

Janiyah hung her head. She knew that she would disobey that order. There was no way she could leave early again tomorrow. Rita had strictly commanded everybody to be there or else. Something big was going down, and she needed all her soldiers on the front line.

***

The dreams were different now, like the Universe was trying to show her something. The night Ronnie died was the same night she had decided to escape Big Sam. They had a big fight before Sam walked into the apartment and convinced Ronnie to let her and the children go. But Big Sam was a liar and manipulator, and Janiyah regretted that night. If she had not tried to leave, they wouldn't have been kidnapped by Sam's driver and brought to the warehouse where Ronnie died.

Janiyah tossed and turned, throwing the blanket off of her and then eventually to the floor as she drifted in and out of sleep.

> Big Sam walks over to Janiyah and rips the tape from her mouth, and specks of blood fly off with it. Sam cringes and wipes the droplets that landed on her hand off on her jeans. Janiyah screams from the pain.
>
> "Please," she cries, "Please don't hurt her."
>
> "It was just a matter of time before you told Ronnie about our little investment. And although I knew you would do it, I do admit it pissed me off. But you led me right where I needed to be."

Big Sam overturns the box handed to her by one of her men and spills the contents on the table. She picks up a nickel-sized baggie filled with a white substance and holds it up to the light. She smiles wide and looks to Janiyah like a female version of The Joker without the makeup. Her eyes even looked like they were blue.

“I call it, trip,” she says, laughing hysterically.

Noise is heard near the front door of the warehouse, and everyone turns to look. Samantha’s men point their guns in the direction of the noise. Ronnie emerges from the shadows, pointing a gun. Big Sam smiles.

“This keeps getting better! I happen to like family reunions.
“What up, Ron? What it do, lil homie?”

Ronnie walks forward, his hands shaking as he keeps the gun pointed at Sam.

“What’s going on Sam?”

Sam raises a brow. “Welp. It kinda looks like big sis got herself in some trouble. But we got this so you can put the gun down.”

Sam’s men have not lowered their guns, and Ronnie is not dropping his.

“Ronnie, please,” cries Janiyah. “Do what she says. Put the gun down.”

“Not until it let’s ya’ll go.”

Big Sam shakes her head. "See, that's your problem. Hardheaded."

She nods toward the men, their guns pointed in Ronnie's face. She signals for them to lower it.

"It's cool, fam. He ain't that stupid."

The men lower their weapons and Ronnie tears up.

"Nah, Niyah see, I made myself a promise."

"Ron, please," Janiyah begs. "Put the gun down."

Ronnie takes his free hand and wipes the tears that fall.

"I promised myself that I would take care of it. I knew it all along. Somewhere in the back of my mind, I knew it. It was all too perfect. But I promised myself that…"

Janiyah turned her attention to Big Sam in a desperate attempt to get Ronnie to lower his gun. "Big Sam, please! He doesn't know what he's saying."

"No, let him talk. He's standing there with his chest all out, probably done sold a lil trip, got some pussy, scraped up enough crumbs to get a lil piece. It's cute."

"At least I actually have balls between my legs."

The men standing around laugh, and Samantha gives them a

threatening look as they attempt to suppress their laughter.

"Yeah, I see you've grown a pair. Looks nice on you. Smell good, too. Now, if you don't mind, we are kinda in the middle of something."

"Yeah, me too," Ronnie says before pulling the trigger.

"Ronnie no!"

CHAPTER TWENTY-SEVEN

Crowds of people surrounded the entrance to Altgeld, music blasted from open windows in one of the top floor apartments. People smoked, drank, and played cards in front of the building. It was Friday, so the church mothers were still at choir rehearsal at the only black church up the street, and the candy lady was open. The excitement was high in the community on payday. The ice cream truck sang down the street, women hung sheets out on the patio gate to dry, and men played basketball across the way at the basketball court. It had been added during the renovations but was nothing more than a parking lot now. The basketball rim had been knocked out and replaced with a crate, the once smooth patio graffitied with slang, curses, and "Rest in Power," in memory of the most recent death. Crack vials also loitered the court. Trip users left potato chip bags, candy wrappers, weed bags, and empty plastic bottles.

Closer to the buildings, girls jumped double-dutch on the sidewalk, and young boys stood up on their bikes, riding them back and forth. The boys wore no shirts, and yellow headscarves hung out of their back pants pockets. Their pants were always sagging, revealing their boxers underneath. They knew they would be scolded by Miss Vicky if caught. She was always telling them to pull their pants up and giving the history of Buck breaking. It was the practice of slave owners raping black men as a form of punishment on the plantations and then forcing them to sag their pants in the fields, so everyone knew the cost of disobedience.

"Nuh-uh," the boys would protest. "I heard that started in the jails, Miss Vicky."

"You heard wrong," the middle-aged woman would protest, "That's not to say it didn't circulate in the jails, but that ain't where it started. Buck breaking was popular in the Caribbean ya see, and it involved white supremacists and slave owners raping a male slave in front of the public to embarrass him and make him feel less of a man. Buck breaking became popular when slave rebellions went up. Enslaved men were first stripped naked and flogged..."

"...what's flogged Miss Vicky?"

"Boy, don't they teach you nothing in school?"

The boys would laugh, holding onto the handles of their bicycle.

"He don't go, Miss Vicky," another boy would chide, laughing at his friend.

"You remember how ya mama beat you for stealing car parts last year? That's flogging. Whoppings. Beatings."

"She flogged ya ass," the boys' friend would tease.

Vicky would hide her laughter and continue her lesson.

"Like I said, they would flog—whoop the man in front of a crowd after they raped him to serve as a warning to other slaves. Sometimes enslaved men with families were forced to have sex with each other in front of their family, or they were raped in front of their sons."

"Dang," the boy would say, doing wheelies on his bike.

"Mmmhmm, sure did. Lot of 'em who had gone through the process of buck breaking killed themselves afterward or ran away and never returned. Better learn ya history."

"Aiight," the boys would say, smiling and riding off. Miss Vicky would go on to finish her laundry. Secretly, they enjoyed listening to her black history stories and would ask her questions just to get her talking. Though, they still did not pull up their pants.

The boys were not regular teens. They were corner boys for Big Sam's crew. The yellow bandanas that hung from their back pockets were proof that they belonged to the organization. Miss Vicky liked talking to them because they were innocent during these conversations. When she spoke to them, she saw their youthfulness peeking out from behind their eyes. It was hard trying to get a fourteen-year-old boy who paid all his mama's bills with drug money and had already decided he was a man to listen to you, but when Miss Vicky told her stories, they listened. At these times, she could see them like she used to when they were just four and five years old before Scar recruited them.

Miss Vicky said a prayer as she stood looking down from the patio where she hung her sheets, thankful there was no bandana hanging from her only son's back pocket. She had raised him to respect himself and others. Unlike many in the buildings, his father was in his life, and she believed it made a world of difference. He could not stay with them, though. The Welfare people wouldn't give her food stamps if they found out she had a man there working—and she needed her stamps. Kenneth ate her out of house and home, so Kenneth Sr. lived in an apartment across town. He sent for his son every so often and sent her money when he could. He wanted badly to move his family out of Altgeld, but Miss Vicky had asked that they wait until after the boy graduated high school.

Kenneth and Victoria "Miss Vicky," Simmons moved into Altgeld in the early 2000s when renovations were new. Miss Vicky had lived in Robert Taylor since 1984 until they tore the last of them down. She didn't want to move from one housing project to another, but lack of finances didn't give them much of a choice, so when word spread of the new Altgeld Apartments,

Miss Vicky filled out an application. Upon approval, she moved into a three-bedroom, two-bathroom apartment with new appliances and even a washer, dryer, and microwave.

"The committee sure outdid themselves!" she would say to her friends.

Miss Vicky was committed to keeping her apartment nice. Of the drugs, gangs, and poverty around her, she refused to be a part of the damage and raised her son to abandon the belief that living in the projects meant he had to fit the stereotypical image of his environment. He did not have to be a gang member, and he did not have to sell drugs. Kenneth did not have to have tons of babies he didn't know or take care of, and their apartment did not have to be infested with rats and roaches.

And it wasn't.

Kenneth Jr. had made it to his senior year of high school. He had a little job and a scholarship from the debate team to attend the University of Chicago. He was smart, and most importantly, to Miss Vicky, he was not in gangs. The people in the building respected him and hung their hopes on his shoulders. Somehow his making it out of the projects meant they would all make it out. Everyone, gangstas included, was proud of Kenny and respected him, which is why she didn't want him hanging around that Janiyah girl.

She shook her head at seeing her and that fast tail friend of hers the other day. The young lady was pretty, but that was the problem. It was the pretty ones you had to worry about the most. Vicky was no fool. She knew the girl dealt with *trip*. Word had it she was a virgin, but Miss Vicky wasn't buying it. She hung around that Tab girl, and everyone knew there was nothing virgin about Tabitha.

"Birds of a feather flock together," she said to the air, removing one of her sheets from the patio gate and shaking it to be folded. The sound of a bouncing ball in the distance grabbed her attention.

"What's that Mama?"

Miss Vicky looked up and smiled. "Hey there."

Kenneth held the basketball in his arm and leaned in to kiss his mother on the cheek, "Hey, Ma."

Vicky looked the boy up and down.

"What are you doing here? Ain't you supposed to be at work?"

Kenny shrugged, bouncing the ball between his legs and then throwing it into the air and letting it twirl on the tip of his finger. He enjoyed basketball as a sport, but he wasn't going to be another basketball player. "There are other things out there for black men to be, son," his dad had said.

"Took off today."

Miss Vicky shook her head, "Again Kenny? Now I done told you I ain't got no money…"

"I know Ma."

"...and the lil money ya daddy sending over here ain't hardly enough to cover the welfare..."

"Ma, I know."

Miss Vicky finished folding the sheet.

"As long as you know I ain't got no money, so don't borrow none. Better take yo ass to work."

Kenny laughed and shook his head, bouncing the ball on the concrete as the sound of an ambulance penetrated the air.

Miss Vicky and Kenny leaned against the gate and looked down from the eighth floor where crowds were forming. A woman screamed, and that set off the cries and shouts of others. Kenny's heart skipped a beat as he watched members of Big Sam's crew wipe away tears, curse, and punch the air with their fists. Brothers hugged other brothers, and some focused on keeping the crowd at bay as the paramedics left the building carrying someone on a stretcher with a sheet covering them. Miss Vicky shook her head.

"Another one bites the dust."

Kenny frowned. "Come on Ma."

"Come on, nothing. Actions have consequences. You reap what you sow. You make a bed; you lie in it. Violence begets violence. Malcolm called it the chickens coming home to roost..."

Kenneth tuned out the sound of his mother's voice as he watched the paramedics lead the body to the truck. He scanned the crowd below, and his heart jumped at the sight of Janiyah and Tabitha. He walked off.

"Don't go down there, Kenny."

"I'll be back, Ma."

"Kenny!" his mother yelled but he had already disappeared down the stairs.

Vicky sighed and returned to folding another sheet when she spotted her son running out of the building and over to those girls.

"She ain't nothing but trouble."

CHAPTER TWENTY-EIGHT

Kenny was out of breath by the time he caught up with Janiyah and Tabitha. Tabitha raised a brow and cut her eyes at Janiyah.

"Hey, Kenny. Ain't you supposed to be at work?"

"I took off," he nodded. "Hey, Niyah."

"Hey."

"You off an awful lot lately."

Kenny ignored Tabitha's suspicion. He couldn't help but notice Janiyah looked sad.

"What's going on? Who got popped?"

Janiyah folded her arms and looked away.

"Scar," said Tabitha.

Kenny lurched back as if something heavy had hit his chest.

"What?"

Tabitha nodded, looking around at the crowds as the ambulance prepared to pull off. "Yep."

Kenny put his hands on his hips and lowered his head.

"Damn."

Tabitha turned to face Janiyah who was wiping tears from her eyes. She knew she had a crush on Scar.

"Hey, girl. You alright?"

Janiyah shrugged. "I'm okay."

Kenny elevated his head. It was early. *What were they doing at Altgeld anyway?*

"What ya'll doing here so early? I usually don't see ya'll till I get off, and even then ya'll leaving."

"Business," said Tabitha. Today was the day of the big shipment and Renita's big news. She had called them in earlier than usual, revealed Scar's death, and commanded no one to leave without her approval.

"Speaking of which, we gotta go," said Janiyah.

"See you, Kenny. Thanks for coming over."

Kenny's heartbeat raced. "You're welcomed."

"Later K," Tabitha said waving.

Tabitha raised a brow as she and Janiyah entered the building and waited by the elevator. Kenny needed to cut it. Janiyah did not like him like that.

"Girl, stop playing with that boy."

Janiyah frowned. "Ain't nobody playing with him."

"I'm just saying. You know how he feel about you. You gotta watch out for them obsessed types."

"Girl, Kenny ain't on nothing."

"You doing okay, though? You been kinda quiet. I know you was feeling Scar."

Janiyah shrugged. "It's not that. I had another dream about Ronnie last night. This time I saw everything play out right before he died."

Tabitha stuck a piece of gum in her mouth. "That's good, right?"

Janiyah shook her head.

"I'm not sure. I mean, I *think* I remember what happened, but it was just kind of strange. It was right when Sam introduced trip, but it was something about her eyes. They were blue."

Tabitha looked down. Janiyah noticed.

"What?"

"Oh, girl. Nothing. Just thinking. That is weird, but you know how dreams are. A lot of shit just be getting mixed in."

"But that's not the only thing. Ronnie called Sam a *it*."

Tabitha blew a small bubble and popped it. "A what?"

"He said not until *it* lets ya'll go."

Tabitha raised an eyebrow. "You do know Sam was gay, right?"

"Yes, but it didn't sound like he was making fun of her in that way. It sounded like he called her "*it*" intentionally. 'Not until *it* lets ya'll go.' Like she wasn't human or something."

Tabitha's cell vibrated in her purse. She was thankful for the distraction. "Now you are starting to sound like ya crazy-ass auntie," she said, digging the phone out and answering it.

Janiyah laughed to ease the tension, but she did not find it funny. *Why would Ronnie call Sam it? And why didn't she remember that part before or Sam's crazy blue eyes? Could it be a glitch in the dream world, or was this what actually happened?*

"'Sup," said Tabitha, rolling her eyes at the sound of the voice. "What you mean you here?"

Tabitha's body tensed up and she looked around.

Janiyah could not know she was talking to Fred. He was besties with Tina, and she was not trying to have Tina in her business. Frederick was a cool friend, and they knew each other for a long time. Even more, the nature of their relationship could not yet be revealed to Janiyah, so she didn't tell her that it was him who had called that day at her apartment before they left to bag.

"Aiight. I'm on my way." Tabitha hung up the phone. "Damn," she said under her breath.

"That one of your boos," smiled Janiyah.

Tabitha shrugged. It was best to leave Janiyah assuming it was.

"Look, I gotta go do something real quick," she said walking back.

"Girl, stop playing. I don't wanna go up here by myself."

Tabitha yelled from behind her, "Imma only be a sec. Tell Rita I'm on my way!"

***

Janiyah's shoulders dropped as she stepped onto the elevator. *What could be so important Tab had to run off like that?*

"I don't wanna go up here by myself," she complained as the elevator car stopped at the fifteenth floor.

Janiyah exited the elevator and walked down the empty hall. That was odd. It was always crowded on fifteen. Janiyah's head turned to naturally respond to men who would usually be calling out to her, but no one was there. Janiyah felt like she was walking the halls for the first time, although she had walked it a thousand times. Goosebumps developed on top of her skin, and she shivered from the eery silence. She did not hear children playing or smell food cooking. For the first time, the apartments on fifteen seemed vacant, so much so she was relieved to see Rita, Moose, and Big Boi standing by the opened door of 1502 smoking weed.

"Aye, where Tab at?"

Janiyah cringed and then turned around to face Rita.

"She on her way."

"She better be. We getting started in five minutes."

Five minutes? Dang.

Janiyah turned and ran back the other way.

"Now where *you* going?"

"To get Tab!"

CHAPTER TWENTY-NINE

Tabitha folded her arms and shook her head.

"What the hell are you doing here?"

Fred stood up from the building he was leaning against, blew a cloud of smoke, and put the cigarette out on the ground and stomped on it.

"Can you even taste that?"

Fred smirked. "Nah, but it makes me feel better."

They were in the back where residents parked their cars but didn't hang out. Fred looked around anyway. He was dressed in all black and wore dark shades. Tabitha frowned.

"And why you look like that for? This ain't the Matrix."

"Got something for me?"

"Jason her man. That's all I know."

"Her man?"

"Yes, and you didn't answer my question. What are you doing here?"

Fred removed his shades and blinked, his eyes flashing blue.

"Because we have a problem."

Tabitha looked around and closed her eyes. When she opened them, they were blue.

"How did you know?"

"I've always known. The Almighty sends us out in twos, or did you forget?"

Tabitha smiled. Fred was right. They always went out in twos: Big Sam and Renita, her and Janiyah, Tina and Fred. Tabitha thought about the good ole days, back before Big Sam turned dark. It felt good to be her usual self for a second. Since Ronnie died, she had been Janiyah's guardian angel, but she did not expect to get so close to the girl.

Fred looked Tabitha up and down. "I like the skin."

Tabitha looked down at herself and smiled.

"Thank you. You don't look too bad yourself."

Fred laughed, "Not bad for a 43,000-year-old, eh?"

"Forty-three? When did you have a birthday?"

Fred frowned, "I turned four last century. You have definitely not kept up."

Tabitha looked around again. They were not invisible and being seen out in public this way was not safe.

"What's so important you just had to see me?"

"Tina's in trouble."

"What else is new?"

"No," said Fred, "For real trouble. Juan has had me spying on all of you."

"Fred?"

Tabitha and Fred jumped at the sound of Janiyah's voice. Fred quickly put his shades back on and Tabitha changed her eyes back to brown.

"Oh, hey girl."

Janiyah eyed her friend. "What's going on?"

"Does Tina know you are hanging out in the projects?"

Janiyah rolled her eyes.

Good diversion!

Tab, no telepathy. Not now. It's hard enough as is to focus.

Fred extended his arm. "Come on."

"What?"

"I'm taking you home. Let's go."

"No. I can't leave."

"If Tina finds out you are here that's yo ass. If she finds out I knew you were here that's *my* ass."

I forgot how funny you are. Haha.

Tab. Enough.

Janiyah folded her arms. "What are you doing here anyway? What's this all about?"

"I'll explain in the car. Let's go."

"And what am I supposed to do with *my* car?"

Tabitha looped her arm in with Janiyah's. "Look Fred, we gotta go."

The women walked off.

"Tina's in trouble," said Fred, stopping Janiyah in her tracks. "They think she's got something to do with the Steakhouse murders."

Janiyah frowned. "What?"

Stop talking to the girl. You are making her think. I got it from here.

"Come on J! We gotta go," said Tabitha, pulling Janiyah away.

CHAPTER THIRTY

Jason sat in the passenger's seat of Eddie's truck and let the wind caress his arm as it hung out of the window. He scanned the area as Eddie pulled up to the front yard of Altgeld and put the truck in park. A few men stood around the building smoking cigarettes and talking, and some young boys rode around on bikes, yellow bandannas hanging from the backs of their sagging jeans, their shirts off on this warm morning.

"Look pretty chill out here today," said Eddie.

Jason opened the car door and stepped out, stretching as he stood outside of the truck.

"It's early."

Eddie laughed, slamming his car door and locking it.

"True."

The men approached the building, speaking to some of the men standing around. Jason pulled out his cell.

"We here."

***

"Okay. We are on our way."

Tina hung up the phone and started the ignition.

"Here we go," she said looking into the rearview mirror. Az had made his body small again and was sitting patiently in the back of the car.

***

Juan looked around at his team, which included Amy, who wore a smirk. Although she couldn't go with them to Altgeld, she had lived for this moment. Tina was full of pride and needed to be put in her place. Although the shutdown didn't have anything to do with Tina directly, she would be affected nonetheless. Word got around that her niece was hanging out at the buildings.

"Our intel has tracked Frederick, who is on-site at Altgeld. It's still early, which means there's not a lot of activity. If we are going to move, we need to do it now. I don't have to tell you how important this is."

The officers shook their heads and looked around; mumbles and whispers filled the room.

"Keep your phones on and your ears open," continued Juan. "When I send the word out to move, that's when we move. Anyone not paying attention will be left behind."

***

Janiyah and Tabitha walked out of the elevator to the patio of the fifteenth floor. No one surrounded the doors of 1500, and only Big Boi stood next to the closed door of 1502.

They approached the door, greeting Big Boi as he searched them. Janiyah frowned. Something about the energy today was off. She shook her head. It could be the dream she had about Ron and blue-eyed Sam.

"Where's Moose?" asked Tabitha.

"Said he had something to do. Whatever it is, he better finish it in the next three minutes."

The women shook their heads and entered the apartment. This time, there were no boxes on the tables, and everyone was fully dressed as they sat around the table like corporate workers sitting in a board room. Janiyah frowned as she and Tabitha took their seats.

"Kenny?" she said, spotting him leaning in a chair on the other side.

"What are you doing here?" she mouthed.

Kenneth shrugged and Janiyah frowned. He looked different than usual.

Tabitha nudged her and raised a brow. "Told you," she mouthed. Janiyah shook her head. *Miss Vicky gonna go off.*

Rita sat in a large recliner chair at the head of the table, and two men stood behind her.

"I know ya'll heard about Scar."

Whispers and curses floated around the room, and Kenny sat up, scowling. Janiyah rolled her eyes at him. She hated he was trying to be someone he wasn't. If she liked him a little before, she didn't like him at all now.

"Trust and believe," said Rita. "His death was not in vain. Whoever did this is already dead."

"That's rights," and "sho-nuffs" echoed throughout the room.

"Besides that, we got other business to attend to. I know ya'll been waiting on this new shipment. It's all we been talking about for the last few weeks, but that shit ain't gonna come."

Tabitha and Janiyah looked at each other.

"We shutting it down."

"What?" Tabitha pretended to be irritated.

Where are you? The meeting has started.

Fred: Meeting up with Tina. She's with Az. Also, Juan is here.

"Matter of fact," boomed Rita's voice. "We moved all product out last night."

Janiyah scanned the room. No wonder it looked so empty coming in.

"What are we supposed to do?" asked a woman.

"Yeah," said another woman. "I mean, some of us got bills to pay."

"We get some kinda severance or something?" asked a man.

Soon, questions shot out from everywhere.

Rita banged her fist against the table. "Shut the fuck up!" she yelled, silencing the room.

"The severance is your life, goddamit. That's what you get to keep. Any product you still got, get rid of that shit today. Look, ain't nobody covering ya'll ass this time."

Tabitha understood how difficult being human could be. Emotions and feelings were all-consuming, as she felt sad for Renita. Her angel had turned dark, which turned her dark. You could do the worst thing to lead your human astray, especially if they had little insight into the spiritual realm. Protect them from hurt, harm, or danger. Redirect, reposition, and adjust. They have the gift of free will, so let them make their own choices. Never deceive or compromise. Those were the rules of the guardian.

CHAPTER THIRTY-ONE

Tina pulled up to Altgeld and stepped hard on the brakes, jolting Az forward. She looked at him through the rearview mirror.

"Sorry."

"It's okay. Wait until you've time traveled."

Tina and Az got out of the car, Az having shrunk himself down to the size of an average man, even shorter than how he'd appeared to Jason. He was only about six feet now.

The once new Welcome to The Altgeld Homes sign was spray painted black with gang signs, and the once vibrant green grass were patches of faded green and brown. Tina watched as two young boys stared at her while leaning against the building entrance, yellow bandanas hanging from the back of their sagging jeans. Tina shook her head and shivered to think Janiyah was spending all of her time here with this Tabitha girl.

"Tina?"

Tina turned around at the voice.

"Fred?"

Fred ran up to Tina and Az, and the corner boys frowned and looked them up and down as they passed them and walked into the building.

***

Jason and Eddie agreed to meet with Moose at Altgeld. They parked behind Tina's car, walked past the graffitied sign and corner boys, and entered the building. The smell of sauteed onions greeted them as Eddie knocked against the door to apartment 809.

"Something smell good as hell."

Eddie smiled. "Told you, bro."

The door swung open, and Miss Vicky greeted Eddie with a hug.

"Hey, Ma," he said, holding her tight. She wasn't his mother, but Eddie referred to her as "Ma," out of respect for his father's ex.

Miss Vicky let him go. "Ya'll come on in."

"What up, boy!" said Moose, setting a plate of biscuits, gravy, beef bacon, grits, eggs, and toast on the kitchen table.

"What it do, boi," said Eddie as the men hugged. Miss Vicky smiled and shook her head as she walked into the kitchen to stir the gravy.

"This my man Jay. Jay, this my cousin Moose."

"What up," said Moose licking his fingers.

Jason nodded. "'Sup," he frowned. He had heard stories about this cat. When Eddie said his cousin at Altgeld, he didn't know he meant Moose, as in one of Big Sam's leading officers Moose. As in blood on his hands Moose.

Miss Vicky untied the apron from around her waist and hung it over one of the chairs near the table they were all standing around.

"Ya'll go ahead and make yourselves comfortable. I'm gonna head to the back and let ya'll talk."

"Thanks, Auntie," said Moose.

Miss Vicky smiled. "You're welcome, son."

Eddie looked around. "Where Kenny at?"

Vicky shook her head. "He better be at work."

"Oh yeah, that's right. He still working at the Walgreens?"

"For now, yes, but he keeps taking time off like he does…"

"…he taking off?"

Moose diverted his eyes. Jason noticed.

Vicky sighed. “He sniffing up behind some heffa got him missing work and such. He better not get nobody pregnant is all I know.”

Eddie laughed. “Okay. My mans got him a lil honey dip. Imma have to talk to him.”

“Please do. He ain’t hardly listening to me, and I don’t know what ya’ll’s daddy over there doing.”

Eddie nodded. He hadn’t seen his pops in a minute.

“Yeah, I’ll holla at him.”

“Okay, well, I’ll leave ya’ll be. Go ahead and eat something now, here?” Vicky put her hands on her hips. “You know, The Panthers had a free breakfast program.”

Eddie and Moose looked at each other and laughed.

“Yeah, I heard about that,” said Jason, who didn’t see Eddie shaking his head. Entertaining Miss Vicky would lead to an hour-long lecture, and they had to take care of this business.

“That’s right,” said Miss Vicky. “That’s where the free breakfast program in the schools come from.”

Jason folded his arms, “Really?”

“Hmm, sho nuff. January 1969, ha!”

“She getting excited,” whispered Eddie.

“Yeah, I know,” mumbled Moose.

Eddie faked coughed. “Aye, Jay?”

But it was too late. Miss Vicky was going in.

“See, it was Bobby Seale that planned the program with Father Earl Neil and Ruth Beckford-Smith, who coordinated the program and recruited neighborhood mothers. The Breakfast Program was a hit!” Miss Vicky clapped her hands together.

Jason laughed. “Dig that.”

“It quickly spread to twenty-three cities by the end of the year, and when it came to Chicago, you know I had to get on board. The way I cook? Honey child, please.”

The men laughed.

“The Panthers fed more than twenty-thousand children nationally in 1969. By 1971, at least thirty-six cities had a breakfast program. The National School Lunch Program administrator had to admit that the Panthers fed more poor school children than did the State of California. Now ain’t that something?”

Jason nodded. “It really is.”

Miss Vicky laughed and walked to the back.

“Man, Auntie know she can talk.”

“She talking some good stuff though,” said Jason.

“Yeah,” agreed Eddie. “Ma real passionate.”

Moose grabbed his plate from the table, and the men sat on the couch.

"What's the word cousin? I hear you need my help."

Jason's jaw clenched, and he cut his eyes at Eddie, who winked back at him. The last thing he wanted was help from someone like Moose. He wondered if Eddie knew what his cousin was into. He had left the A long ago. *Was he still hip to the game?* It didn't seem like it.

CHAPTER THIRTY-TWO

All black police vans pulled up to Altgeld, and the corner boys scattered like roaches to blinding light. Men wearing all black jackets with yellow FBI letters on the back jumped out of the vans, their guns pointed in all directions. Dozens of them surrounded the building, some running inside and some running to the back. Young fourteen and fifteen-year-old boys were snatched up and wrestled to the ground.

"Man get off me!" they screamed as the cuffs scratched against their skin.

Juan sat in one of the vans with Officer Parks and Officer Jones. They watched the activity from monitors streaming from the cop's body cameras and the hidden cameras Fred had installed around the building.

"At least he did something right," murmured Juan.

***

Renita stood up and walked over to the window and watched in horror as cops and FBI agents manhandled her young soldiers. The voices of the cops could be heard on the floors below them, kicking in the apartments of residents.

"Fuck!"

"Oh my God," said Janiyah holding hands with Tabitha as the room panicked and the weakest members bolted for the door. The women stayed glued to their seats. As expected, Kenny was by their side within seconds. This time, Janiyah didn't mind.

"What the hell is going on?"

People fell all over each other trying to get out of the apartment, and then the room went dark.

"Whoa, what the…"

Renita stumbled backward. She couldn't see anyone around her.

"Tab!"

"I'm right here. You holding my hand, bitch."

Usually, Janiyah would laugh, but she couldn't see her hand or Tabitha or anything in front of her. It was the pitch-black you only see in the country after the sun sets, and there are no streetlights or stars.

***

"Before Mama died, she and Pops was first loves and shit. It was cool at first. I had everything a fly-ass three-year-old could have," Eddie laughed and dapped up Moose.

Jason shook his head but said nothing. Instead, he devoured the last of his grits and eggs while Eddie explained his and Moose's connection.

"But then Moms got hooked on Dad's product, and it was all downhill from there. She started leaving me with Moose mama, who was super cool."

Moose smiled, "We used to get into some shit, boi!"

They laughed and slapped hands three times.

"We were struggling big time at my house. My breath was stanking, pants flooding. I ain't have a pot to piss in or a window to throw it out of."

The men laughed.

"Moms hooked you up though," said Moose.

Eddie looked at Jason, "While my mama ran the streets and Pops chased her, Moose mama was my mama. Everything he had, I had. She ain't make me feel like I was different or nothing."

Jason swallowed food. “That’s why ya’ll call each other cousins?”

“Yup,” said Moose.

Eddie nodded. “And then when Pops said he was about to have another baby, I was too pissed off. Like nigga, you can barely take care of the kid you got. By the time lil Kenny came along, Dad had cleaned himself up and moved out the A. I was jealous as shit.”

Jason nodded. He could understand that.

“But Miss Vicky was real cool about it, though. She made it easy for me to like her. I used to think she talked too much.”

“Used to?” smiled Moose.

Eddie lowered his voice. “I still think she talk too much.”

The men laughed.

“But she was cool about letting me spend the nights, and she let me babysit Kenny sometimes. He was a crybaby, but it was cool.”

The men laughed again but then the apartment went dark.

“Oh, my Lord,” cried Miss Vicky, running into the front room. “Ouch!” she screamed, slamming her foot against one of the chairs near the kitchen table. “ComEd better not play with me ‘cause I know I paid that bill.”

"You alright, Auntie?" Moose shouted, turning his head in all directions.

Jason stood and tried to feel his way to the kitchen table. Miss Vicky screamed again, and everyone jumped at the crash of glass that shattered on the floor. Jason turned in the direction of the sound. Moose must have dropped his plate. The entire apartment was pitch black. The sound of glass continued to reverberate throughout the apartment as pictures fell from walls and the house shook.

"We gotta get out of here," said Jason, feeling around.

"This way. I got the door open. Come on!"

Eddie frowned in the darkness. "Now, Auntie, how you know where the door is?"

Miss Vicky made a face she wished they could see. "I've been living in this building longer than most of ya been alive. I know this apartment like the back of my hand. Now stop all that lollygagging and come on. Let's go."

Jason shrugged and surpressed a laugh. "Yes, ma'am."

CHAPTER THIRTY-THREE

Tina blinked as they climbed the stairs. She tried to open her eyes only to realize they were already open. The darkness was oppressive and heavy, and a wave of nausea struck her. Tina stumbled on a stair.

"Az!"

Az activated his blue light, which shone from his eyes like two flashlights piercing the darkness. Tina closed her eyes at the brightness. She needed to adjust to the sudden change.

"Sheesh, Az. Tone it down a bit."

Az turned to look at Fred, who had also activated his light.

"Open your eyes," said Az.

"Okay but turn it down some. Are you trying to blind me?"

When Tina opened her eyes, the entire stairwell was lit, and it felt like the room was spinning. It only lasted seconds but felt much longer. When the spinning stopped, she turned to see that Az and Fred were holding her up. Dizzy and disoriented, she looked around, and Fred's eyes were blue.

"What happened?"

"You almost fainted," said Az.

Tina looked into Fred's bright blue eyes.

"Am I dreaming? Is this a dream?"

"Don't worry," said Az. "He's one of us. He's here to protect you."

"What? Fred, what's going on?"

"It is true."

Tina shook her head. "I don't know what's going on, Az, but this is *not* the time to be joking. Turn his eyes back so we can go. I'm pretty sure Jason's here now."

"T, it's me. For real."

Tina rolled her eyes. "Of course, it's you. She turned to look at Az. "How did you do it? Can you turn my eyes blue, too?"

"Tina, Fred is one of *us*."

Tina held her hands out in front of her and leaned against the railing. Although there was light, her eyes still struggled to adjust. She felt like she was losing her balance. After tonight, she's never taking sight for granted again.

"Not the Frederick who's been my partner for five years."

"I'm a little more than that, Tina."

Tina's head pounded. "I need my meds."

"T, don't panic."

Tina looked Fred up and down and rolled her eyes.

"And don't take the medication," said Az. "It will dull your senses, and you won't be able to complete the mission. You won't be capable of developing your light."

Tina sat on a stair and put her head in her hands. Fred had been around her long enough to know what was happening.

Az, that's enough. She's overwhelmed. We still have work to do before all can be revealed.

"Come on T," said Fred in the voice she was familiar with. "Paschar and her legion are here. We must get to Jason and Janiyah before it's too late."

"Janiyah?"

Fred saw the shock register in Tina's face. She was so stunned to hear Janiyah's name that it had not even registered how he knew Paschar. Fred decided to let it slide. There was no more time to sit around talking.

"Yes, but don't worry. She's safe."

A sound struck their ears like an alarm had gone off. Only this alarm was a woman's voice. Tina quickly covered her ears at the streaking.

"Ah!" she screamed, holding on to both her ears. "Stop. Make it stop!"

Fred lifted Tina and threw her over his shoulder. He would have to carry her the rest of the way.

"We have to go," said Az. "She's here."

***

"Shit, shit, shit!"

Officer Parks rolled her eyes at the sound of Juan's voice without trying to hide it. No one could see, dark as it was.

"We were *extremely* careful this time. How did they know we were coming?"

He said it more like a statement than a question.

"I guess Fred's the snake we thought he was," boomed Officer Jones's voice.

Officer Parks nodded in the darkness. Fred's the only person who could have known they were coming. He had to have alerted Big Sam's crew, and they shut off the electricity. She felt her way around the van.

"I know one thing. We can't stay in here all night."

The three fumbled around the van, feeling their way to the door. Parks rolled her eyes again.

"Juan!"

"What? What's wrong?"

"You know that's my ass."

"Sorry."

Jones laughed. "C'mon ya'll. I got the door open."

The three climbed out of the van without much hope of light. Not only were the lights to the building out, but so were the streetlights. Most night skies were the darkest of greys, but this one was pure black. It was like someone shut off the stars and moon. The three held their hands out in front of them, feeling around like blind men swallowed up by nothingness.

Parks tripped, and covered her face, in preparation to hit the concrete.

"Whoa!"

She pushed against what she had landed on, punching and feeling it.

"What the?"

As her hands felt around the cotton fabric, she touched skin.

"Eww!" she jumped up, bumping into Juan.

"What is it?"

"I think I just fell on a body."

Juan shook his head in the darkness. "Shit."

Officer Jones sighed. "Man, it's gotta be some light around here somewhere." He felt around to his back pocket, pulled out a towel, and used it to cover his mouth. "And what is that smell?"

***

The siren stopped, and Janiyah lowered her hands from her ears. Tabitha shook her head and put her fingers in her ears, feeling wetness.

"Yo! My shit bleeding!"

"Tab, calm down."

"How you gonna say calm down, J? What the hell is going on?" Tabitha laughed on the inside at her pretentiousness.

Kenny dropped to his knees. "I got an idea. Come on."

He pulled Janiyah down with him who pulled down Tabitha.

"Kenny what the fuck?" she complained.

"Let's crawl to the door."

"It's dark as fuck."

"Tab, stop cussing, damn," said Janiyah.

I see you are still overplaying your part.

Tabitha rolled her eyes at Fred's voice in her mind. It was hard pretending to be human, let alone a human teenager.

Try being twenty-thousand-years old in a seventeen-year-old body and see how well you do. Besides, I've done a lot of studies. Young humans curse a lot.

They don't curse that much.

Yes, they do.

"C'mon let's go. The door is this way," said Kenny.

Shh. Gotta go. You got Tina?

Yes.

"Nigga, how you know where the door at?"

You also use the N-word a lot.

I said Shh!

"Because everybody going this way, and I feel a draft. Come on."

The three crawled on the floor. Kenneth was in the lead, with Janiyah behind him and Tabitha behind her. They maneuvered around the few people still in the apartment.

"That's my hand motherfucker! Shit."

"Tabitha, really?"

"What? So, I'm just supposed to let somebody step on my hand? They know what they doing."

Janiyah laughed. "No, they don't because it's dark…"

"Oh, snap!" said Kenny, raising his arms to cover his eyes. The beaming blue light struck the darkness like lightning. The sudden change from dark to light was blinding.

Took ya'll long enough.

Everyone but Tabitha covered their eyes as the light illuminated the apartment.

Janiyah peaked from behind her hands.

"Auntie?"

***

Fred lowered Tina to the ground when they made their way to the fifteenth floor. The light from Az's body illuminated the patio, and they could see the opened door of 1502. Fred turned his eyes back to their human color as they made it to the door.

"Niyah?"

Tina ran into the apartment, and into the arms of Janiyah. Tabitha and Kenny stood to their feet and looking around saw others had been on their knees also.

"I'm sorry. I'm so sorry."

Tina caressed Janiyah's head. "It's okay."

Janiyah turned away from Tina to face the people in the apartment. Everyone had their mouths open and their eyes wide with shock, and for some, fear.

Tabitha winked at Az.

Hey, long time, no hear from.

I've been busy.

Fred shook his head at Tabitha.

You need to let that go.

And you need to mind your business.

Janiyah turned in the direction of the light and saw what everyone had been staring at. Seeing the fear in her eyes, Tina turned quickly to face Az and Fred. She had forgotten about them standing there, and Az's eyes were still burning blue light.

CHAPTER THIRTY-FOUR

"Hey guys, check it out." Officer Jones pointed to the bright blue light coming from the building.

"What is it?" Juan asked the question to no one in particular. The more they stared at it, the brighter it got, and they had to look away. Soon, they could see around the building. Officer Parks gasped at what they had been standing in the midst of, covering her mouth with her hand. The light revealed bodies of FBI agents and corner boys spread out over the lawn.

"Oh my God."

Officer Jones covered his mouth. "Now we know what that God-awful smell is."

The three looked around, scanning the bodies on the ground.

"Come look at this."

Officer Parks pointed to the body of a young boy. It was like a skeleton with a thin layer of skin, and his eyeballs protruded outside of the sockets. It was similar to the dead bodies found around the city.

"Big Sam's crew is good but they ain't *this* good."

The sound of thunder crackling in the dark sky made the three look up. The clouds moved in a swirling motion, the silver hues flashing highlights of pink. Attacks of lightning struck the concrete in the middle of the road, splitting it in two. A tree collapsed, and the deadweight smashed the top of someone's car. Car alarms rang loud, and the thunder continued to strike the air. Chairs left outside were now being tossed from one end of the street to the next. The wind picked up and howled like a thousand hounds. Officer Parks, Jones, and Juan stood in a frozen state of fear, the sounds so loud it sent vibrations pulsing through their body. Officer Parks squinted her eyes as she covered her face because the wind was so strong it made breathing hard.

"Is…is that a horse?"

The clouds were swirling faster now, and figures started to appear, followed by laughter as the sky turned a myriad of colors. The rain came next, hammering the ground and striking the building like bullets. The three covered their heads and faces.

"Quick inside!" yelled Officer Jones.

They ran into the building and the lobby. As usual, the hall was a mess. A broom that looked like it could add dirt to the floor instead of sweeping it away lay across the floor, and a curtain rod that looked like it belonged in someone's bathroom leaned against the one window. The window itself was covered only by a white bedsheet, and someone had also left only one of the three armchairs put there during renovations, and it was missing a leg. Parks contemplated sitting but leaned against the wall instead.

***

The blue light from Az's eyes had now illuminated the entire building. Miss Vicky frowned.

"Now ain't nobody said nothing about no blue lights," she shook her head as she thought of the committee. She did not remember hearing anything about blue lights being installed in the buildings.

The wind continued to howl, and the rain now sounded like hail had begun to fall. Jason, Moose, Eddie, and Miss Vicky descended the stairs. They could hear windows breaking and the mischievous laughter of a woman's voice.

Miss Vicky paused before taking the next step.

"What on Earth in all the world?"

Eddie held onto her hand, and Moose and Jason walked behind them. Jason kept an eye on Moose. He still didn't trust him far as he could throw him.

Moose lifted up his shirt to reveal a forty caliber.

"I stay strapped."

Jason shook his head as the laughter grew stronger, closer.

"What *is* that?" The sound was irritating him.

"Man let's hurry up," said Eddie, guiding Miss Vicky to the next step, but she snatched her hand back. It was no longer pitch black.

"I am not disabled."

Eddie forced a smile, but his constant roaming eyes and the sweat sliding down the side of his face indicated he probably needed to hold Vicky's hand more than she needed to hold his. The group walked down the stairs, and as they approached the main level, Jason swatted at a fly, and then Miss Vicky swatted, then Moose, and then Eddie. They all seemed to be fighting the same insect and then, more laughter.

"What's so funny Miss Vicky?"

"That wasn't me, Hunny."

More laughter as they continued to swat at the fly. Jason looked at it more closely.

"What the hell?"

The fly looked like a tiny woman with wings. She was six inches tall, slim, and her skin was creamy pale. Even though Az's light provided illumination, the creature's glossy golden hair, shimmering wings, and skin like whipped milk made it clear you could see her even in the darkness. She winked at Jason, wiggling her long, slender nose and long, pointy ears as she swerved in and out, around and around, laughing with a voice that wasn't as tiny as her body.

Miss Vicky held onto her chest. "I think I'm having a heart attack."

Moose clapped his hands into the air, trying to squash her, but she was too fast.

Eddie punched the air.

"Man, what are you doing?" Moose laughed. Eddie looked ridiculous trying to punch the fly.

"What *are* you?"

The creature slowed in the air, swerved in, and sat on Miss Vicky's shoulder.

"Get it off! Get it off!"

The creature shook her head. "Calm down, lady. It's not you I want." She winked again at Jason and raised a brow.

Moose frowned, pointing at the tiny woman.

"What. The. Fuck. Is. That?"

"Not what? *Who*?" the tiny woman shrugged.

Jason thought back to his conversation with Tina and her alien friend. He still had his doubts until now.

"*What* are you?" he asked again.

"Hi," the creature extended a tiny hand. Jason frowned and she pulled it back with a wave.

"Suit yourself," she put her hands on her tiny hips, her wings wagging with excitement like the tail of a dog.

"I'm Goo. Your favorite fairy."

Goo winked and Eddie thought he would pass out.

"This isn't happening right now. Fairies aren't real."

Goo lifted herself from Miss Vicky's shoulder and sat on the other one, closer to Eddie and folded her arms.

"That's mean. I am very much alive."

Before anyone could see it coming, Moose slapped the place where Goo had landed, her tiny body falling down flat.

"Ow!" Miss Vicky held onto her shoulder, rubbing it. Moose forgot that swatting the creature also meant punching Miss Vicky in the arm.

"Not now you ain't," he said, proud of this victory. "Got yo ass."

"Eww," whined Miss Vicky as she let the tiny body roll off her shoulder and onto a stair.

"Is it dead?" asked Eddie.

Jason looked down at the fairy and shook his head, "I don't think so, but I'm not staying here to find out."

The others followed Jason down the stairs leading to the main floor.

Eddie tilted his head. “She look Japanese to ya’ll?”

CHAPTER THIRTY-FIVE

"Guys, this is Az. He's an angel and he's here to help us."

Kenny frowned. "A what?"

"Come on. We have to go."

"We definitely should not split up. They always do that in the movies, and it never works out," said Kenny as they ran out of the apartment.

They were all so distracted by Az that they had not noticed the silence that settled over the building like a blanket. All the people who had run out of the apartment screaming were gone. As they ran down the patio, Kenny stopped in his tracks as if hitting a brick wall. He fell to his knees and covered his face with his hands. Running closely behind him, Janiyah also fell back.

"Ahh!" she screamed, stumbling backward.

Tina fell into Fred's waiting arms, and Tabitha held onto Janiyah as they stood on the concrete patio and the humans hid their faces.

Kenny, Janiyah, and Tina turned away from the light and kept their hands covering their faces. The light was so intense they had not even paid attention to the creatures it shone from or noticed the myriad of colors as they trembled.

Az, Fred, and Tabitha exchanged glances. They knew they had to do something. The humans would not survive in the presence of the four.

Tabitha thought about activating her blue eyes. If Janiyah was a target, she needed to be protected.

Stand down.

It is my job to protect her.

You will lose her.

Tabitha rolled her eyes, but she knew Fred was right. Guardians of teens must not make it known to their young humans that they are their guardian angel. The mind has not yet matured, and they could lose them and be assigned to a different human. No angel wanted to be reassigned. It can take years to establish a connection and relationship. Janiyah had to be at least twenty-five years old before Tabitha could reveal herself. One human year was a thousand angels' years. *Only eight thousand more years to go.* The guardian sighed.

Four large men who looked like Az surrounded them, all emitting a different light. But unlike Az, these men had wings and were covered with eyes all around, even under their wings. Each held a seal in its right hand and stood surrounding the group like an army.

"They are here to help," boomed Az. "These are the four living creatures sent by the Almighty. They are each holding a seal and opening the seal will release a different weapon. Each emits a different light."

One of the four creatures stepped forward, raised his arms, lifted the seal into the air like a trophy, and began to unfold it. As the beast opened the seal, a wind gushed by, and the ground shook beneath them.

"Aunt T!" Janiyah yelled in fear as the three women hugged.

After a moment, everything stopped, and the angel who broke his seal stood back. None of the other angels moved, and no one spoke.

***

Moose pulled out his gun as soon as they made it to the main floor.

"Holy shit," said Eddie ducking his head as a creature flew over him.

"Don't just stand there. Help us!"

Officer Parks screamed as she swung the broom at the all-black creature who looked like a large bat with wings.

Jason ran over to the three-legged chair and kicked the rest of the legs out.

"Here. Take this," he said giving one leg to Miss Vicky, one leg to Eddie and keeping one for himself.

The creature laughed in a woman's voice and dipped low enough to pluck at Juan's head as Officer Jones picked up the curtain rod and slammed it against the creature's body. It stumbled a bit but didn't break stride. The beast jumped back into the air, flapping its black wings, and growled.

Miss Vicky stood close to the wall, holding on tight to her chair leg.

"What the heck is it?"

"Shoot it! Shoot it!" yelled Officer Parks noticing Moose's gun.

"It's a gargoyle," said Jason. "It must have been sent here by Paschar."

Eddie ducked, swinging his chair leg as the creature flew over them. "Who the hell is Paschar?"

"The head demoness witch trying to kill us," said Jason, swinging.

Officer Jones stepped closer to Moose. "Shoot it!"

"I can't! It keeps moving!"

Jason shook his head. He knew Moose was all talk. That's how it usually was. The loudest ones in the room were usually the weakest ones in the room.

"Don't I know you?"

Juan recognized Moose but couldn't tell from where. He ran with Big Sam's crew. He was sure of it.

"How did you do it?"

Moose looked at Juan.

"What?"

"What's the trick here?"

Moose frowned. "Trick? Are you serious? This look like some gang shit to you?"

"So, you *are* in a gang."

Officer Jones shook his head, swinging at the laughing gargoyle as it flew above their heads and then finally landed down the hall.

"Juan, really?"

Parks rolled her eyes. Something supernatural was going on for sure, but Juan had his head so far up his ass he couldn't see it.

"Stop being a cop Juan. Jeeze."

"Aww, look at that. I love good old fashioned human conflict," the gargoyle's wings flapped.

Eddie leaned closer to Jason. "Why they all sound like women?"

Jason shrugged.

"Because we *are* women."

Jason raised a brow. "We?"

"Call us Legion because we are many."

The group looked around at each other.

"We are not talking to a gargoyle. We are not talking to a gargoyle. We are not talking to a gargoyle," repeated Eddie to himself.

The creature's body jerked like it was seizing, and Miss Vicky shut her eyes tight. Whatever was happening, she didn't want to see it. Everyone else stood back and cringed at the sound of crushed bones as the beast changed. Its ligaments were stretching, and they could hear the organs shifting. The large body shrunk as it transformed, and in seconds the gargoyle had transformed into the body of a beautiful brunette.

"What the…" Moose stumbled back.

The woman looked down at herself and smiled, her heart beating fast. She remembered the first time she shifted. It was much more painful and took days for the transformation to take place. Paschar warned them not to shift too much as it depleted their energy source. Some people got midway through the shift and never fully transformed. They walked around half-horse and half-woman until they died. The only exception were the demigods who were born that way, half-human, half-animal from angels who mated with the beasts of the land.

"I look much better in person."

"You sure do, Hunny Bun!"

Everyone turned their heads at the familiar voice and Jason frowned. "I knew that bitch wasn't dead."

"Sasha!" screamed Goo, swooping in and sitting on the shoulder of her Legion sister.

"Goo?" asked Miss Vicky watching the fairy.

"How do you know its name?" asked Parks.

Eddie pointed. "We met her in the stairwell."

"Sheesh how many of them are there?"

Goo pointed at Moose, unfazed by the gun in his hands.

"You hit me."

“Shoot the damn gun!” Officer Jones was getting irritated because he and Parks had left their guns in the van.

“I had not been hit that hard in centuries.” Goo tilted her head. “Well, no. That’s a lie. I was hit pretty hard last night.”

Goo and Sasha laughed hysterically.

“Come on, Moose! Shoot her! Do it now before she turns back into that thing,” said Eddie.

“It’s gone.”

“What’s gone?”

“The gun. The gun is gone!”

Jason lowered his head. “Shit.”

“Flimsy little thing,” said Sasha, walking toward the group with Goo on her shoulder, twirling the gun around her finger like it was a toy.

Outside, lightning flashed across the sky, and thunder roared as the building’s walls and the floor trembled. Miss Vicky screamed as the quake knocked the group down on the floor. The intensity also knocked Sasha back.

“Whoa, whoa, whoa!” screamed Goo as she flew off Sasha’s shoulder and was flung to the end of the hall. Sasha shapeshifted back into the beast, snarling in anger at the force that knocked them down.

The door to the entrance of the building swung open, and a gust of wind blew in. Jason, Officer Jones, and Eddie tried walking toward the door to close it, but the wind was too strong. Rain and an avalanche of hailstones fell from the sky.

Sasha barked at the door like an angry rottweiler but would not come close to it. Officer Parks exchanged looks with Miss Vicky as they sat on the floor against the wall. Hailstones began to gather at the door's entrance as the three men tried unsuccessfully to reach it and close it.

"Close the door!" yelled Juan.

Eddie wiped the rain from his face, fighting the wind with his hands. It felt like they were outside.

"What do you think we're trying to do!"

Goo began to sing which pierced the group's ears.

"Ahh!" yelled Officer Parks in frustration. The singing sounded more like screams.

"She's going to bust my damn eardrums," cried Moose covering his ears.

As Goo screamed her siren, Sasha marched forward but tripped and fell back on her own tail. Something was stopping her from coming close to the door and she was not as strong since she shifted. She growled and barked some more, showing teeth like sharp knives.

"Something's coming," said Jason, backing up from the door.

He pulled back Jones and Eddie.

"Hey fellas, get back! Get back!"

The group heard a thunder of hooves get closer to the door and froze at the sight of a white stallion.

"This can't be real," murmured Eddie.

He who sat on the horse looked like Az, except his body looked like it had been painted white. His eyes were white lights, and he wore a gold crown on his head and an arrow in his arms. The horse's muscles rippled from under its powerful legs as it neighed.

The rider pulled back on his bow, striking Goo in the chest. The group cried in astonishment.

"Didn't see that coming," said Jason, amazed at how such a large arrow could pierce such a small creature.

"Those can't be normal arrows," said Miss Vicky.

The group watched in wonder as the creature shot arrows out like darts into the gargoyle's body. Sasha growled and marched forward but was unable to move. The horse roared and stood up on its hindlegs.

"Whoa shit!" said Moose as the group backed up.

"I'm gonna throw up," whined Juan. "I can't look," he said, facing the wall.

The rider with the arrow guided the horse closer to Sasha, and the horse breathed fire from its nose. Sasha screamed and writhed in pain as her beastly body burned.

A voice boomed. "Do not be afraid."

"Az?" yelled Jason.

They could hear Az's voice in their ears but could not see his form.

"We are getting our asses beat down here, man!"

"Who is Az?" asked Officer Parks.

The horse walked over to the group, but the rider with the arrow never changed his stature. He pointed his hand toward the group, his bright eyes like headlights.

"Hey, watch where you point that thing!" yelled Moose.

"What's going on man?" asked Jason into the air.

"A seal has been loosed."

CHAPTER THIRTY-SIX

Az, Fred, and the four living creatures held hands and they all lifted their arms into the air.

"Fred, no!" screamed Janiyah. She turned to face Tina. "What is he doing?"

But Fred did not respond. Instead, his eyes flashed blue as they raised their arms into the air and stood still like statues. Tabitha mentally rebuked the spirit of jealousy she felt creeping into her mind. It had been many centuries since she could openly show her power.

As the angels stood in solidarity, a liquid substance materialized and covered Janiyah, Tina, Kenneth, and Tabitha like a cloud on every side until they were in what looked like a living dome.

"No way," said Kenny watching the shield cover them like the top of a bowl. He poked his finger at the liquid bubble.

"It's cold."

"Aunt T what's going on?" cried Janiyah watching Fred look like he was possessed.

"It's okay. I'll explain it later."

Kenneth pulled Janiyah close. "I got you."

If you say so, thought Tabitha.

Janiyah leaned into his arms. She would typically pull away from him, but she was hysterical, and his arms were comforting.

"This will protect you from the power of our presence," boomed Az. "Do not go outside of this protection, or you will not survive the intensity."

"Wait," Tina stepped forward, looking up at Az from the dome. He and the creatures looked taller than they did just a few seconds ago. She wasn't sure what had happened with the loosening of that seal, but something did. She had to look up at Az even more. Even Fred was taller, which was a lot creepier since she was used to his human form.

"You want us to stay in here?"

"If you want to live, yes. No one can hurt you inside this shield. This is your protection," Az did not move from his position in the circle. "When our power is activated, we are intense on the human body. My human form made it easier for you but combined, our energy can kill you unless you stay inside the protective shield."

"Well, well well, the gang's all back together," laughed the voice of Paschar.

Kenny, Janiyah, and Tina looked around in fear.

"It is time. Stay inside the shield."

"Stay inside the shield," mocked Paschar, laughing.

"Show yourself."

"Why? So, the gang can release their seals on me? I know the game."

"This is crazy," cried Janiyah.

"I know one thing," said Kenny, "I'm not about to sit inside of a bubble."

Janiyah quickly glanced his way. "Kenny, no. You'll die."

"Oh, come on. Don't tell me you believe that crap."

Tabitha shook her head. This was exactly why young teens could not meet their guardians. Their belief was not mature enough. "There are angels right outside this shield. What's not to believe?"

And an angel standing right in front of you.

"Angels we don't know are here to harm or protect us."

"At least someone's got some brains," said Paschar. "Come on out, guys. The weather is fine!" she laughed as a cold wind gushed by, shaking the protective shield.

"I can break that thing, ya know."

"Don't listen to her," said Az. "Deception is her greatest weapon."

Janiyah shrugged, "Didn't the blue one say this shield will protect us?"

"And it will," said Tina. "As long as we stay inside."

Kenny waved his hand and folded his arms. "I have a headache." He thought about his mom and wondered how everyone else in the building was doing. They couldn't have all evacuated. Where was everyone? Shouldn't the cops be here by now?

***

"A seal?"

Miss Vicky frowned. "Like the Book of Revelations seal?"

"I don't think it's that kind of seal, Auntie," said Moose.

"Then what kind of seal is it? Lord, we living in Revelations. It's the apocalypse."

"I doubt that very seriously," said Juan.

"Then what is it then? Somebody tell me what the heck is going on here. Why is a voice speaking to us from God knows where, why is a fairy and gargoyle trying to kill us, where is my son, and where the hell is that horse?"

Miss Vicky shot the questions out in one breath. Jason walked over and rubbed the woman's back.

Everyone looked around.

"Yeah," said Eddie. "Where *is* that horse?"

The white horse and its rider were nowhere to be seen, and no one remembered watching it ride off or vanish.

"We need to get out of here. The van is still outside," said Officer Jones.

Eddie looked down the hall at the large beast still lying on the floor with arrows sticking out of its body and shivered.

"You think they really dead?"

"I doubt it," said Jason. "We not fighting flesh. We fighting spirits."

Officer Jones waved. "Man, let's at least get out of this building."

The group gathered and walked closer to the door, and Jason lifted his shoe from the floor. "What the heck," he said looking at all the water on the floor. "I don't remember the floor being this wet."

"Yeah, ain't that much rain come in," said Eddie.

As they inched closer to the door, a wave of water poured in like a Tsunami, knocking them back. It was so much water the group found themselves swimming around the Altgeld lobby. Moose floated down the hall near the elevators, and Juan floated down the stairway.

"Guys! Guys!"

"Aye, that's Juan," said Jason. "He over there by the stairs!"

"I got him," said Officer Jones, swimming his way.

As Moose struggled to swim his way back to the group at the other end of the hall and Officer Jones rescued Juan from washing down the stairs, Hitomi floated through the door. She knew that if she showed her complete image, they would be afraid, so she stuck to the half-human and half-mermaid look. She also did not want to deplete her energy. It was something they always teased Sasha about doing. She would shapeshift and then have to hunt for blood to get the energy back. Only Paschar could change without losing much power, but Paschar was a savage who feasted on more souls than any of them. Either way, shifting often was not a smart strategy for the rest of the Legion.

"Don't worry."

Everyone looked around in amazement.

"Is that a mermaid? Like, a real mermaid?"

"Don't trust it bro," Jason said to Eddie.

Hitomi understood why they wouldn't trust her, but it was Paschar she was betraying. Scar had softened her human sensibilities. She did not understand these human emotions completely, but she knew that not all humans were flawed. She justified her feeding by only eating the bad ones, like men who raped their women and children.

"Please," she said ushering them to the door. "We don't have much time. She already knows I'm here."

Moose made it down the hall and spit water out of his mouth.

"Well, well, well," he said, smiling. Jason shook his head.

"*Who* already knows you're here?" asked Officer Parks. "And *who* are you?"

"Look, I'll explain later. Please, come on."

"You guys can stay here and meditate on it, but I'm going with the Mermaid lady," Moose said, swimming toward the door.

Jason frowned and Eddie shrugged.

"Dammit," Jason said swimming behind Moose. What choice did they have? Seeing Jason move influenced the others to follow. Everyone swam toward the door until the waters began to recede and they could walk out of the building.

"I don't trust this," said Officer Parks.

"Me either, Hunny."

Parks cracked a smile. She liked this Miss Vicky.

The group walked out of the door, their bodies feeling heavy as if they too were filled with water. On the dry ground outside, they marveled at the damage of the storm. Household appliances from stoves to chairs were sprawled about, and several cars had filled the hole in the ground where the thunderstruck. The block looked like a hurricane had swept through it.

Juan and Officer Jones finally made it out of the building, and Jones rushed over to the van. He really wanted to get his gun. Even though Moose's proved irrelevant against the powers they were fighting, having it made him feel better.

Everyone else stared at Hitomi as she floated in the air.

"I can explain."

Moose licked his lips, but Hitomi ignored it. She was used to getting this kind of reaction from the male humans. If they were not friends of Scar's, she would have had that one's soul by now.

Jason folded his arms.

"My name is Hitomi. I'm a friend of Scar's.

Moose frowned, "Scar?"

"Yes, Scar. We were…friends."

Moose cocked his head back. The mentioning of his boss had him on edge.

"Scar as in Sean Scar? Sean Carver Scar?"

Hitomi sighed, "Yes."

"Do you know who killed him?"

Officer Parks shook her head. Juan just could not grasp anything beyond being a detective.

Officer Jones joined the group, with a smile on his face, while adjusting his waist.

"Look," continued Hitomi. "This will probably go over your heads." Hitomi paused to see the annoying facial expressions. She didn't care. She still thought angels were superior to humans. She would do this favor in Scar's memory, and then she was back to feasting on the souls of those she didn't know. Her emotions weren't that deep.

"Big Sam was never human."

"What are you talking about?" Moose was irritated now. Hitomi ignored it. She would probably eat him later.

"We have observed you for centuries, hiding among you in plain sight. We are journalists, news broadcasters, actors, celebrities, politicians, and yes, even rulers of drug empires. In the seventies we decided to step it up with crack. It didn't take off until the eighties, and boy, did we have a ball in the nineties!" She smiled at the memory. "We sent Big Sam to run the Chicago operation in 1984 at The Robert Taylor Projects. Boy, did we have fun at that place. Things slowed down when the 2000s hit, though, so we had to come up with something else."

Jason scratched his head. "But there is one thing I don't get. If you are angels and you are so powerful, how come you die?"

Hitomi's eyes turned red with rage, and her once gentle demeanor vanished as her voice grew deeper.

"That's none of your business." She didn't want to admit that gods die like men and are imprisoned in a place called Tartarus deep beneath the Earth. Paschar didn't have any real power. None of them did. They were angels, but they were fallen angels.

The sky crackled with thunder and the clouds swirled above them. Hitomi looked up.

"She's here," she said, snatching Jason by the wrist, his body dangling in the air.

"Aye, put me down!"

"Jay!" yelled Eddie.

"I'm sorry," roared Hitomi. "I have to take him, or I couldn't save any of you."

Officer Jones put a few rounds in the air, trying not to shoot Jason. One bullet hit Hitomi's tail as she floated higher into the sky. Jason screaming from above.

CHAPTER THIRTY-SEVEN

"There is a spiritual and physical side to all things. First is the spiritual. It is the higher realm. Things take place there first," said Az.

"Blah, blah, blah," whined Paschar. "Get to the good parts. Talk about me," she laughed.

"Today," continued Az, "Their weapon is trip."

"Get the fuck outta here," waved Kenny.

"Wait, what?" Janiyah stood next to Tina and looked up at Az. She was used to his physical appearance now.

"What do you mean that weapon is trip?"

"He *means* Big Sam was one of mine," laughed Paschar. "She worked for me. They *all* work for me."

Kenny cut his eyes. "Nah. That ain't true. She's lying."

"Oh? He's one of mine, too."

Tina turned to face Kenneth. "What?"

Kenny shook his head. "She's lying. Didn't Az or whatever his name is say deception is her greatest weapon? She's lying."

"And *her*."

Tina turned to face Janiyah, fury in her eyes.

Although Paschar could not be seen, there were only two women in the dome besides Tina, and everyone knew about Tabitha. The guardian read Tina's aggressive energy toward her and laughed to herself. The only high she and Janiyah's customers got was a sugar high. That's what she had turned their bags of trip into when they worked. As Janiyah's protector, she could not allow her to contribute to Paschar's scheme.

"Oh, so you dealing trip?"

Janiyah covered her face. "I... I didn't know."

Paschar laughed.

"Do not fight. You are feeding her."

Tina covered her mouth. "Oh my goodness. It's you."

"I'm sorry, T," Janiyah whined.

Tina shook her head, "No, not that. We'll talk about you selling drugs later."

Janiyah lowered her head to hide her smirk. It wasn't a funny situation, but her aunt could be corny.

"No, the connection," Tina faced Az. "It's true, isn't it? Janiyah working for Big Sam's people is the connection attracting Paschar's legion."

"Yes," boomed Az. "But there's more."

"More?" Tina held her head. It was pounding.

"Wrong," mocked Paschar. "All you have to do is tell them. Enough with the riddles. How sneaky."

"Okay. If all this is true, why didn't anything happen?"

"What are you talking about?" Kenny was starting to get on Tina's nerves now, too.

"The 'seal' was broken, but nothing happened. Didn't he say that releases some weapon? Well? Where the weapon at? Huh, blue guy? Where's the weapon?"

"Just because you didn't see what happened does not mean nothing did."

Kenny waved Az off and inched closer to the water-like substance, teasing it with his finger.

"Feels like water. You really think this is protecting us? All he been doing is sitting around here talking."

"I agree," laughed Paschar. "You may as well come out. You can all come out."

Paschar laughed and sang as another one of the living creatures, one different from the other, stepped forward.

Kenny chuckled. “Here we go. Let me guess, another seal?”

The creature raised his arms into the air, and the eyes all around him blinked as he began to unfold it. The living dome shook again, and the group gathered in the middle and huddled. This time Kenny didn’t join as he braced himself and the ground shook beneath them.

“I’m not dying inside no bubble.”

***

The holes covering the ugly creature before him reminded Jason of The Matrix people who weren’t born in the free world. The large black wings were almost as tall as their owner, each long feathery wing flapping with excitement. Jason shivered, saying nothing. The high altitude made it hard to breathe, let alone speak.

“I can see you are uncomfortable,” said Paschar, morphing back into the beautiful black woman Jason first saw her as. Besides, Tina and Janiyah were arguing down below, and it was filling her up.

Although in her human form, Paschar kept her wings. They were beyond the clouds now, and as Jason’s oxygen levels decreased, he was losing consciousness.

“Good job,” said Paschar, pretending to clap.

Hitomi smiled. “I told you I’d get him.”

"Indeed, you did."

Paschar eyed Hitomi and nodded at the blood on her tail.

"Oh," said the mermaid, shaking her head. "It's nothing. Amazing, they still don't know how to shoot. What with all Hephaestus's work." Hitomi laughed nervously, and Paschar smiled weakly. As a smithing god, Hephaestus made all the weapons of the gods in Olympus. He served as the blacksmith of the gods and was worshipped in the manufacturing and industrial centers of Greece, particularly Athens. Between Chicago's gun violence and mankind's never-ending fascination with wars, Hephaestus was definitely getting his. Paschar respected that. What she didn't respect was Hitomi's betrayal. She stretched the human arm beyond physical capacity so that it wrapped around Hitomi's neck like a snake.

"Please…Pas...please," Hitomi cried, scratching her nails against Paschar's snake-like arm as Jason's body floated in the sky.

"What did we talk about?"

"I... I can't," Hitomi struggled to loosen Paschar's grip.

"This is the second time that you have disobeyed my orders, and now the four are at Altgeld."

Small yelps escaped Hitomi's mouth, and tears welled up in her eyes at the mention of the four living creatures. They were still connected to the Almighty Power. Their presence meant The Legion could not even come close to the rest of the humans.

"Why did you have to kill him?" Hitomi spoke telepathically.

Paschar's grip hardened, and she growled at the mention of Scar's death.

"Your weakness for the humans may have cost us the war. Your services are no longer needed," she said, letting the mermaid go and watching her fall below the clouds, screaming on the way down.

"Pas! Please!"

Paschar dusted her hands off and smiled at the unconscious Jason floating in the sky.

***

As the group argued, the negative energy built up, and the building shook violently. The doors to the apartments on the floor swung open. Tables, chairs, sofas, refrigerators, and other household appliances and equipment rushed out of the house and floated in the air. Some of the items crashed into the dome, and it felt like it had moved an inch. "Az!" yelled Tina as they all screamed and gathered in a tight huddle. Even Kenny held onto the sides of the dome now, his hands sinking in and out of the water-like liquid. He had to admit it was amazing that he could penetrate the liquid bubble with his hands but the appliances that crashed against it couldn't. Az read his mind.

“We control everything outside of this shield with the power of the Almighty. Nothing can penetrate this protective space. But the choice you make inside the shield is yours. If you want to leave, nothing will stop you. But remember, leaving offers you no protection from what is outside.”

Tina and Janiyah were in awe of the appliances spinning around in a circle above them, too overtaken by fear to worry about Kenny.

The living creature that had stepped forward continued to unfold the document. As he broke the second seal, the appliances fell from swirling in the air and crashed against the concrete. Although nothing could break through the dome, the noise caused the group to jump and cover their heads. The appliances hit the ground and broke into several parts scattered on the patio, and Kenny dipped his hand into the liquid shield.

“Kenny!”

Tina had tears in her eyes this time as she watched half of Kenny’s arm hang outside the protective space.

“Kenny, please. Don’t do this,” cried Janiyah.

“Kenny, come on. Stop playing,” Tabitha said in her best-worried-teen voice. Although she was an angelic being, she could not interfere without transgressing the rules of the guardian. *Let them make their own choices.* As angels, they also had the gift of choice. That is how some could choose to fall, like Satan or, more recently, like Big Sam. Free will seemed a blessing and a curse.

Kenny smiled. "Chill out. I'm not gonna do anything. You should feel it, though. It's like being underwater."

Kenny snaked his arm back and forth outside of the dome and did the same with the arm inside of the dome.

Janiyah folded her arms. "Kenny, this isn't funny. Pull your arm back in. Come on."

Kenny waved. "Look at ya'll. Scared," he laughed, pulling his arm in, but it wouldn't move.

"What the heck?"

"Kenny, what's wrong?"

He looked up and Janiyah could see the fear in his eyes.

"I can't. I can't move my arm."

"Come on, help me," said Tina rushing over and pulling Kenny's other arm.

"I can't move my arm!"

Janiyah and Tina pulled against the part of Kenny's arm still inside of the dome. They could tell he was terrified now.

"Tab, come on!" yelled Janiyah, but Kenny was not her assignment, so there was nothing Tabitha could do. She could not interfere with his free will choice. She would have to pretend to be shocked by fear. The guardian commanded her tear ducts to produce water, and the tears streamed down her cheeks.

"Why are you just standing there? Help us pull him in!" Janiyah was screaming at this point and the sound of hooves against the concrete made everyone jump.

"Oh. My. God."

Tina's mouth fell open at the sight of a horse, but it was unlike any horse she had ever seen. This horse was fiery red, and the creature who sat on him looked like Az, but his body was painted red and in his hands was a sword.

"Come on!" screamed Kenny, his voice shaking.

"Kenny hold onto my arm! Hold my arm!"

"He's not moving," cried Janiyah. "His body's not moving!"

"It's like freaking stone," said Tina.

The red horse and its rider marched forward full speed.

"I don't wanna die! I don't wanna die!" Kenny cried, and Tina and Janiyah screamed as they pulled his arm, the sound of the hooves drawing closer.

As the red horse and its rider got close to the shield, the rider pulled out its sword and sliced off Kenny's arm as the rest of him fell back into the dome.

Tina and Janiyah fell back with Kenny since they were holding onto him as blood squirted from his arm socket.

CHAPTER THIRTY-EIGHT

"No!" Janiyah screamed, and she, Tina, and Tabitha rushed over to Kenny as a ridiculous amount of blood poured from his wound. As for Kenny himself, he had passed out.

Tina cradled Kenny's head in her lap. "We gotta stop the blood. It's too much blood!"

Janiyah took off her shirt and wrapped it around Kenny's arm like a tourniquet, and the shirt quickly soaked with blood. Janiyah was now only in a sports bra, and Tabitha wanted to joke about how Kenny would love to be woke for this, but she held back. This kind of thing was traumatic to humans. Certainly not something they would find funny. She spoke telepathically to Fred.

What are we going to do? He won't survive this, and I can't step in.

The four can.

Tabitha was relieved to hear Az's voice in her head.

You cannot step in, but the four were sent by the Almighty to help. They can heal his wound.

Tabitha thought a moment. There was always a stipulation.

But?

But healing him doesn't mean his arm will grow back. It means he won't die, but he will have to live without an arm as the consequence of his choice.

Janiyah's voice broke the human silence and cut the angel's conversation short.

"Why? Why did you have to do this to him?"

"He did it to himself."

Tina frowned at Az's comment. "What?"

"My instructions were clear. Stay inside the dome and live. Go outside of the dome and die. Kenneth made his choice."

"See," said Paschar. "I would never do such a thing. I mean sure we feed on humans, but the process is fairly gentle. We certainly do not cut off arms. How savage."

Janiyah directed her fury at Tabitha, grabbing her by the collar and shaking her.

"Why did you just stand there?"

"I'm sorry J," cried the guardian. "I'm sorry."

She pushed Tabitha against the wall of the dome and fell down on the floor. Janiyah screamed and cried, banging her fists against the dome.

As Janiyah cried, one of the four stepped forward and raised his hands into the air. As he unfolded his document, a ball of fire appeared inside the dome.

"Whoa," Janiyah jumped up and ran over to Tina as they both stood back. Tabitha also stood next to the duo, squinting her eyes and smiling. She knew exactly what was going on. It was the healing fire.

Fire can heat and cook food or burn down a house to humans, but the fire was a force of destruction, creation, and purification in the spiritual realm. The ancients recognized the raw power of fire, who infused this element with prayer, intention, and reverence. In the spiritual, *trial by fire* was not only meant to suggest going through a tough time to come out refined, but the fire could literally, as in Kenny's case, be used to purify and cleanse. The same was true for water which also acts as a conduit that links the two worlds, making it easier for the spiritual and physical to coexist. It was why the dome looked and felt like water. It was not only a dome but a portal.

As the orange and red flame grew and the heat radiated throughout the dome, it covered Kenny like a cloud. As the fire consumed Kenny's body, two more of the four stepped forward.

"Wait," Paschar's voice was nervous. Even she couldn't survive several seals being broken at once. "I have your friend."

"Jason!"

Tina cried out as they watched Jason's body dangle in the air outside of the gates of the patio. If he fell from the height of the fifteenth floor, he would die.

The last two living creatures stepped forward. The thunder growled, and the sky darkened as Paschar's pale skin and feathery wings became visible, and Az teleported Tina outside of the shield.

"Auntie!"

"It's okay," said Fred. "She won't die. This is her time."

"Fred, what's going on?" Janiyah had forgotten all about him and no one had answered her question from earlier. Tears streamed down her face. "You're one of them, aren't you?"

Tabitha pulled her human into her arms and rocked her.

"It's okay, girl."

Meanwhile, seeing what happened to Kenny caused Tina to panic as she stood outside of the shield.

"Az!"

Tina touched her chest, arms, stomach, face, head, and legs. All of her was still there.

“Time for what? Az, what is it time for? Am I going to die? Am I going to burn? Put me back inside the shield thingy!”

Inside the dome, the fire was dying down, and Kenny’s body was becoming visible again, but he was still unconscious.

The four, Az, and Fred, stepped forward, held hands again and surrounded Tina.

“Az. Az!”

“Relax.”

Paschar laughed as she lowered Jason’s body.

“He’s falling!” yelled Janiyah. “She’s dropping him!”

The angels touched Tina’s shoulder, and bolts of light shot out of them and into her as she cried out in pain.

“Az!” cried Janiyah, covering her face as Tina’s body weakened.

Tina writhed in pain as each angel gave her a portion of its power. Everything hurt, and her skin felt like it was on fire. Everything burned down to her fingernails and toes, and she felt her blood had become acid. As Tina continued to cry out in pain, her hair turned white, and her eyes became sockets of light.

When the angels stepped back, Tina was a ball of light. Her entire body shined as she glided toward the patio, burning an opening in the gate with her eyes.

"She's going to fall!" screamed Janiyah as Tina's foot stepped over the ledge.

"She won't fall," said Fred. "This is her time."

The light shot from every part of Tina's body and lit up the sky as she walked on air toward Paschar and Jason.

Meanwhile, the fire had burned out on Kenny. He lay there looking normal as before, covered in blood and with one arm.

CHAPTER THIRTY- NINE

"Damn!" screamed Eddie, tears streaming down his cheeks. What are we going to do? How we gonna get him back?"

The group was still standing around outside of Altgeld, trying to come up with a way to get Jason back. Since they were on the ground, they were not affected by the angelic war taking place above them.

Miss Vicky sighed and lifted her head to the heavens. She did it to say a prayer, but there was something in the sky.

"What in all the world?" she said, pointing up. She never knew her prayers to be answered so quickly.

The group looked up to see a ball of light moving across the sky. Officer Parks covered a part of her face to see better.

"What *is* that?"

"Not another angel I hope," said Eddie.

Juan squinted. "Is, is that a person?"

"Not walking on air, it ain't," said Officer Jones.

Eddie shook his head. "Probably another angel."

"No, not the light, that!"

The group followed Juan's finger to the body hanging in the air.

Moose frowned as he struggled to see. "What?"

"It's Jay!" yelled Eddie.

Officer Jones squinted his eyes. "How can you tell?"

"I don't know but I'm pretty sure that's him."

Officer Parks pointed to the disfigured-looking creature standing next to him.

"And what the heck is that?"

***

Janiyah had to look away and keep her head down, and Tabitha made sure she did. Even inside the dome, the hallway was as luminous as the sun. Together Az, Tina, and the four creatures glowed white and emitted electromagnetic radiation that melted the metal patio gate like wax and shot balls of fire that pierced Paschar's angelic skin.

"Cowards," she screamed, dropping Jason lower as a blood and fire mixture dripped from her body. Paschar ducked and flew around in the sky, dodging the burning light.

***

Eddie, Moose, Juan, Miss Vicky, Officers Parks, and Officer Jones watched the array of white light in the sky on the ground.

Juan lowered his head and addressed the group.

"What ya'll think it is?"

Before anyone could respond, a bright point of light moved rapidly across the sky and descended, crashing somewhere in the distance.

"Oh, shit!" Moose said, covering his mouth.

The ground shook beneath them as everyone held onto one another, and a glowing trail of smoke twirled heavenward.

Officer Parks held onto Officer Jones as she stumbled.

"Was that a shooting star?"

"Man, this shit crazy," said Moose."

"Look!" Miss Vicky screamed, pointing to the sky. "It's another one!"

Another flash of light fell from the sky and crashed in the distance. This time, it set a tree on fire. Before the group had time to recuperate, more flashes of light fell from the sky, crashing to the ground.

"Yo. It's raining fire," said Eddie.

Officer Jones turned in the opposite direction. "We gotta go."

"Look, there's another one!" screamed Officer Parks.

The group ran in the opposite direction of the building, away from Altgeld, as the meteor shower got stronger and stronger, setting everything in its path on fire.

"Whew chile," Miss Vicky said, stopping her short-lived run and putting her hands on her knees.

"Come on! Come on!" yelled Officer Jones, running with everyone behind him.

Officer Parks stopped to look back. "Wait, Miss Vicky!"

The group stopped running to see Miss Vicky with her hands on her hips, breathing hard.

Another bolt of light fell from the sky and tore into the Altgeld building like someone in the heavens was holding a gun and had just fired a shot. The part of the building that struck immediately went up in flames.

"Yo!" said Moose, ducking.

Juan squinted his eyes as he looked down the street at the partially burning building and the now-leaning FBI van where they had just been standing. “It’s getting closer.”

“Just keep moving,” said Officer Jones taking off running again.

The sight of the burning building brought Miss Vicky to tears. So many people trapped inside—so many memories.

To people like Miss Vicky, Altgeld was much more than a project building filled with all the stereotypes usually associated with those who lived there. It had once been a thriving community of black people excited to move away from Chicago’s slums and into a better future. An apartment in Altgeld meant a home where a mother could raise children, cook delicious meals for her family, and a place where memories lived. To watch it burn…that was hard.

The woman walked as fast as she could, with Officer Parks helping her along as another bolt of light fell, hitting another part of the Altgeld building. The fire swelled, and it was spreading quickly.

***

Above, the intense power of light continued to pierce Paschar’s skin, weakening her, and Jason’s body fell like a dead weight, moving quickly toward the ground as Paschar vanished beyond the skies.

As Jason's body moved through the air, the ball of light that was Tina moved even faster, catching him before he hit the ground.

With the power of Az and the four still pulsating through her being, Tina could not feel her body. She seemed only to be floating as she carried Jason's body in her light.

CHAPTER FORTY

The sun came as if it had missed the sky and peaked over the clouds and settled itself over the city. Chicago was loud with the fire's buzz at Altgeld. The fire department, news reporters, police, and dozens of residents, now homeless, stood around in shock at the horror of the previous night's events. No one could say for sure how the fire started that left half of the building dilapidated.

Tina sat on the outside of an ambulance covered in a blanket, and Jason lay on a stretcher on the inside.

"I can't remember."

Az nodded. "That's normal."

"Will I see you again?"

Az looked around at the reporters and the many people spread over the lawn of Altgeld. He had made himself invisible and the size of a normal man again.

"Every now and again."

Tina smiled, remembering how she would see him hanging around the club or popping in and out. She turned to glance at Jason.

"Is he going to be okay?"

"He's fine. You saved his life."

"I don't know about all that. It all seems so surreal. It's like last night was some lucid dream. All I remember is clarity like I had never felt before. My whole body breathed, and instead of walking with my legs it felt like I was walking with my eyes."

"Yep, that's how they say it feels."

"They?"

"Other humans. Other chosen."

"You telling me this has happened before?"

"It happens all the time."

Tina shook her head.

"The war isn't over. It's never over. Somewhere in the future, Paschar will reemerge or another version of a Paschar, and there will be another Tina and Jason. You will see me from time to time, but they won't remember a thing."

Az nodded toward Janiyah, and the other residents in the distance.

Tina turned to look at Jason.

"Will he remember?"

Az shook his head. "I'm sorry."

Tina's shoulders dropped and she sighed.

"Why is it I am the only one who remembers?"

"There is a reason the spiritual world is invisible to the physical world. The two must be kept separate so that you could live your life. Can you imagine how crazy it would be right now for you to see the angels, both righteous and wicked alike, who are walking around right now?"

Tina looked around in a panic. "You mean now?"

Az nodded. "Always now. Always here. The spiritual and physical world operates simultaneously. You can't see the spiritual realm as we can, and we can't interfere in the physical world without permission from the Almighty. But there are times when our worlds touch, such as the opening of portals and doorways."

"Like Ronnie and Big Sam."

"Like Big Sam and Keisha."

"What?"

Tina looked around. She had to remember no one saw Az. She didn't want to be thrown into anyone's mental institution.

"What does his mother have to do with this?"

"Think about it."

"Come on, Az," complained Tina as she sat thinking. *All I know is Big Sam got Keisha hooked on that stuff.*

"That is correct," said Az reading Tina's mind.

"Oh my God."

"I knew you'd figure it out."

"I always thought it was crack, but it was trip, wasn't it? Did Big Sam get Keisha hooked on trip?

Az nodded. "When Ronnie teamed up with one of ours, Big Sam, and he killed her, which had not happened in many of your years, it merged our worlds. But the real connection was established before Ronnie was even born. He never told Janiyah, but Ronnie figured out his mom was the first user of trip. Ronnie realized she had been Big Sam's experiment. He found out about it and went to the warehouse to kill her."

Tina's heart sank. "But they killed him instead."

"Yes, but he did it. Ronnie was successful. He managed to take down a strong entity. Not only did they kill Ronnie, but Ronnie had also succeeded in killing Big Sam, who wasn't human in the first place, sending her angelic spirit to Tartarus and attracting Paschar's Legion to his family. But you should not look at Tyrone White as a victim. In the spiritual realm, among the righteous angels. He is a hero."

"Oh, Ronnie," was all she could say.

"Sometimes you will notice things, Deja Vu, small coincidences. Something will spark now and again, but it will happen in the time it was supposed to happen. Jason will understand everything in the time he is supposed to understand it."

"I finally get everyone to see what I see, only for them to go back to thinking I was crazy."

Az looked up at the sky. "I wouldn't worry about that."

Tina watched as Azbuga walked away, strolling down the street like he didn't have a care in the world, his hand touching shoulders and watching people swat at their backs.

Tina laughed. *Bully.*

CHAPTER FORTY-ONE

A corner boy stopped his bike in front of Janiyah and Tabitha, who were standing in the middle of the street like a lot of other people and draped in a blanket. Someone had given Janiyah a shirt so she didn't have to stand there in her bra.

"Yo, what happened?"

Tabitha shrugged, "A big-ass storm, a big-ass bust, and a big-ass fire on fifteen."

"Word?" he raised his head. "That's ill."

"Yup. Aunt T saved the day, though. Got a lot of people out," said Tab nudging Janiyah.

The corner boy looked around at the cops and detectives.

"Aye, I'm out ya'll," he said, riding off before either of the young women could give an official goodbye.

Janiyah smiled and waved at his back, and uneasiness crept over her face. She looked over at Tina sitting by the ambulance and then at Miss Vicky arguing with some police officers about why they needed to take a statement from her instead of letting her ride in the ambulance with Kenny, who had been rushed to the hospital because of his arm. How he had lost it in the fire didn't make sense to her.

"I don't know. Something's off. What do you remember after Rita said we were closing up?"

Tabitha looked over at Juan, talking to the reporters and Fred standing next to him. He winked, and Tabitha smiled. Part of her was glad everything was back to its normal routine for her human who she still couldn't reveal her true identity.

"Don't know. Don't care. The way it looks out here, I'm just happy to be alive."

"You seen Rita?"

Tabitha was happy Janiyah had changed the subject.

"Nah. I don't know what Imma do about this shut down. You know I need that money."

Janiyah nodded. She still had money from Ronnie's case, but Tab hustled to pay bills, and since last night's bust and fire, the Altgeld hustle was over.

"I could loan you a couple dollars."

Tabitha frowned. "What I look like to you, a charity case?"

Janiyah laughed and threw her hands in the air. “Just trying to help.”

“A bitch just gonna have to go legit. Damn.”

Still cursing I see.

Tabitha smiled at Fred’s voice.

Beat it, Fred.

You are really good at this teenage thing, by the way. Very impressive.

“Working is not so bad, you know,” said Janiyah interrupting Tabitha and Fred’s telepathy. “It’s a Walmart by my house hiring.”

Tabitha turned her attention to the reporter. “Look like Juan ready for his close-up.”

Janiyah smiled. “Always gotta have the credit.”

“I know right?”

Janiyah directed her attention to the argument in the distance. “Look like Miss Vicky giving them the business.”

“She gonna give Kenny more than that if she finds out he dealing trip.”

“I mean, we don’t really know if he dealing, though.”

“Like I said, the more I teach you, the dumber you get.”

Janiyah laughed.

"But she probably won't find out. You know Vicky thinks he Mister Innocent."

"A lot of people got caught in the apartment during the raid though," said Janiyah. "I'm not even sure how we got out."

She's doing a lot of thinking. Shut her down.

Fred was right. It was not yet Janiyah's time.

"True," she said waving. "But I'm guessing Aunt T and Fred."

Good diversion.

I learn from the best.

***

Jason cleared his throat, and Tina climbed inside of the ambulance and sat on the seat facing the stretcher. White bandages covered Jason's neck and wrapped around his face, exposing his nose, eyes, and mouth. Tina touched him gently.

"I'm so sorry, Jay."

"It's…" he cleared his throat. "It's okay."

Jason's eyes darted around, and Tina looked around too. Her heart raced, fearing Paschar was back.

"What?"

"You're…you're not hurt."

Tina relaxed but frowned.

"No. I'm good."

Jason forced a smile. "No more texting and driving for me."

"Driving?"

Everything has been reset.

Tina frowned.

Az? Az, what's going on?

At first, she could only talk to Az through devices like the GPS or when he showed himself. Now, Azbuga was in her head.

One of many gifts of the light.

I see.

Miss Bernice is still watching Kayla and Michael, Amarie is with Jason's parents, and he is not hurt because a group of fallen angels tried to kill him. Jason is hurt from the car accident. You did not just hit his car in this version, but you two ran right into each other, flipping his vehicle.

"What!"

Jason jumped, and Tina remembered he couldn't hear Az's voice in her head.

"Oh, sorry."

Jason smiled.

"So, we still on for that date?"

CHAPTER FORTY-TWO

Three Months Later

The sun was shining like the first day of spring in September, and the wind moved the vibrant green grass in steady waves. There was something about the day, the children running back and forth as they played, some jumping around in the inflatable bounce house and others playing tag. Older men stood over barbeque grills and talked smack while their women laughed at them behind plastic cups. The younger men and women sat around card tables and played spades and dominoes, tipsy and feeling good.

Jason watched Tina from a distance, Amarie by his side.

"Still ain't hit that yet, huh?"

Jason turned to the sound of Eddie's voice.

"You crazy, man," he laughed as they hugged and gave a pound.

"You alright, though? Want me to hold your phone?"

Jason laughed. "You funny. I feel good though. Just happy to be out that damn hospital."

"I feel you, bro. Hey, lil momma. Give me some," he said, holding out his hand to Amarie. The four-year-old smiled big and slapped the man's hand.

"That's what I'm talking about," he turned his attention to Jason. "Not bad, huh?"

Jason looked around the park. Everyone seemed to be enjoying themselves, and the donation boxes were filling up. Moose turned out to be a good organizer, after all. Grant Park was perfect for a community fundraiser. It was the second one since the fire. First, they had to bury Big Steve, whose murder was still unsolved, along with his other friends. People still talked about the funeral, which was huge. Everyone came out, including Jesse Jackson, Al Sharpton, and several celebrities. He even met a man named Barack Obama who said he was thinking of running for President. Jason smiled at the thought. *A black man as President of the United States? Yeah right.*

"Not bad at all."

"Told you we could pull it off again. Told you, bro," laughed Eddie.

"Calm down. I said it was aiight."

"Man, whatever," Eddie nodded over to Tina. "You better go talk to her before Miss Vicky get over there."

Jason laughed, glancing over his shoulder watching Miss Vicky set the table for some kids. Standing next to her was Kenny, in a sling. Jason shook his head. He still couldn't believe how he had lost an arm.

"Yeah, you right. Imma holla at you later, aiight?"

***

Tina found a bench to sit on to absorb the beauty of the joyful community from a distance. She straightened her back and ran her fingers through her hair as Jason and Amarie approached. *Get yourself together, girl. He has seen you before. Or has he?*

Yes, said Az voice. *You two have met. That has not changed.*

Outta my head Az!

Having powers wasn't like it was in the movies, all fun, and games. Tina's senses were sensitive since her experience. She could communicate telepathically with Az and hear conversations from long distances—like when Eddie had asked if Jason had hit that. Tina felt guilty for wishing he would. It was annoying, though, hearing everyone talk at once. She had to really concentrate on focusing on her own thoughts. It was why she carried earplugs and why she couldn't stay for the fundraiser. She was only here to drop off her donation. Word had it that she and Fred helped get people out of the building before the fire, and the attention got eyes on the department and a promotion for her.

Jason smiled as he approached the bench. He looked down at Amarie, who was holding on tightly to his hand. He bent down and held both her hands in his.

"I want you to meet someone."

Amarie shrugged. "Okay."

Tina smiled. *She's adorable.*

"Marie baby, this is Tina and she's a really good friend of mine."

Amarie looked at Tina and waved. "Hi."

Tina smiled. "Hi! You are so pretty. I love your shirt!"

"Thank you. Daddy, can we go to the jumpy thing now?"

Jason stood and laughed. "Yes, Baby. We can go in the jumpy thing." He turned his attention to Tina. "Thanks for coming. We really appreciate it."

"Of course."

Jason raised his shoulders and twisted his body around in a silly way. "Wanna play with us?"

Tina laughed. "I wish I could, but I gotta go. Promised the kids I'll be home for dinner."

"You sure? The jumpy thing is really fun."

"Dad! Come on."

"Oh, which reminds me," Tina stood, dug in her purse, and pulled out the check.

"You know you don't have to do this."

"Boy, take this money."

"If you say so," laughed Jason, with Amarie pulling his arm.

"Text me!" he said, running behind Amarie.

Tina smiled and raised a brow as she walked off, making sure to switch her hips. *I sure as hell will.*

CHAPTER FORTY-THREE

"Okay, ya'll. Let's make it," Janiyah shouted upstairs as the doorbell rang. Michael and Kayla bounced down the stairs and argued over who would sit in the front seat of Miss Bernice's car. Janiyah couldn't believe how big the kids were now compared to when Ronnie first died. The thought of him made her sad, as usual. How she wished he was here.

"You did it last time," whined Michael.

"So, what?" said Kayla, rolling her eyes. "I'm the oldest."

"First of all, neither of you are sitting in the front seat," Janiyah said opening the front door.

Kayla was old enough, far as she was concerned, but not by Tina's standards. Kayla had to be at least twelve before she would bend. "The Centers for Disease Control and the National Highway Traffic Safety Administration recommend keeping children under aged thirteen in the back seat. I am lenient enough giving you until twelve. Why do you think the seat belt can barely fit you? That's not by accident," Tina lectured. She would have a heart attack to discover Mike was anywhere near the front seat. Janiyah smiled and shook her head. *Ole boring by-the-book ass.*

She opened the door, and Bernice's face looked like she'd been caught stealing cookies from the cookie jar. She heard everything behind the door.

"Hey, Miss Bernice." Janiyah, let the woman in. She still didn't understand why Tina had hired a nanny. *Well, at least she's a black nanny.*

"Hey, Niyah. How are you?" she asked, giving Janiyah a hug.

"I'm fine Miss Bernice. They ready for you."

"Miss Bernice!" sang the children as they ran into her arms. She was like a second mother now having spent so much time with them. *And they liked her at least*, thought Janiyah.

"Okay, I gotta go. Everybody good?"

Kayla and Michael shook their heads. They knew when their big sister asked if everyone was good, that meant if they were okay, but it was more than that. After everything they endured, "Everybody good?" told more than if they were okay at the moment. It meant if they were safe, unharmed and if they were not being forced into anything. Were their bodies good? Was their babysitter good? Were they good when she was away? "Everybody good?" meant, "Is *everything* good?" It was their secret code. A code that even Tina didn't know. They had lost one sibling, and Janiyah was going to make sure they didn't lose another one. She smiled, grabbed the keys to her Jeep off the counter, and headed for the door.

"Oh," she said, one hand on her hip.

"You be having them sitting up front Miss Bernice?"

Bernice cast her eyes to the side and blushed.

"It's okay. I won't say anything. Just make sure they are buckled up real tight okay?"

"They are in good hands," Miss Bernice reassured.

Janiyah smiled and closed the door behind her.

"Okay little people. Which one of you told your sister?"

Janiyah laughed to herself, listening to Bernice scold the children behind the door. She unlocked the doors to her car parked on the street and removed her cell phone from her purse at the ping of a new text.

Tina: Omw

It was good having Tina around more often. Since the fire, Janiyah was now working at Walmart with Tabitha. It wasn't anywhere near as much money as they were making with Rita, but at least she could still save. Although the Altgeld operation was no more, word on the street was Rita was trying to rebuild.

Janiyah was enjoying her freedom from it all and didn't want to take any chances. Besides, she enjoyed being able to see Tabitha more and hang out like other seventeen-year-olds. Tina even extended Janiyah's curfew since she was responsible enough to get the job and she was going to college next fall. As not to burden Miss Bernice, Tina also promised to always make it home in time to make dinner for the children, and so far, she had not missed a night. Janiyah smiled. Her eighteenth birthday was also approaching. It was so good having everything back to normal again.

Janiyah: Ok!

As Janiyah drove out of the driveway and to a stop light, she waved at a young woman waiting by the bus stop. Her beauty was extraordinary and for a moment, Janiyah envied her but not in a bad way. The woman was strikingly beautiful with the kind of skin you only saw in the movies. She looked to be about sixteen years old, and her skin was the darkest brown, almost blue-black with not a scar on it, smooth. The girl looked like an Ethiopian with her slender nose and silky, straight, jet-black hair. Janiyah waved and smiled again as the light turned green. The girl at the bus stop waved and watched the Jeep speed off. She smiled and winked as her brown eyes turned blue.

Thank you for reading my book!

It would mean a great deal to me if you could give me your opinion by leaving an honest review of this book on whichever platform you choose. Not only will this let me know what you feel about my writing, but potential readers will also value your feedback.

Thanks!

Other Books by Yecheilyah

I am Soul (poetry)

My Soul is a Witness (poetry)

Renaissance: The Nora White Story (Book 1)

Revolution: The Nora White Story (Book 2)

Stella: Between Slavery and Freedom

Stella: Beyond the Colored Line

Stella: The Road to Freedom

Keep Yourself Full

www.yecheilyahysrayl.com

www.ingramcontent.com/pod-product-compliance
Lightning Source LLC
Chambersburg PA
CBHW020525310726
48979CB00014B/2222/J

* 9 7 8 1 7 3 4 9 2 4 1 3 8 *